TANGLED WEB

By

YOLANDA BUICK

ISBN: 978-17333229-1-1

Memory of:

My Mother

Bessie L. Carter

1939-2015

~Acknowledgements~

I would like to thank, Susan Mary Malone of Malone Editorial Services, Author Phoenix Williams of Delphine Legacy Media, and Jennifer Buchar for being my Beta Reader.

To my Family and friends for your encouragement along the way. Many do not realize the journey involved to bring a finished product. There are a lot of distractions, speed bumps, and discouragement, but with positive people, those distractions are minimal. Thank you for being by my side.

~Yolanda~

Table of Contents

CHAPTER 1

Alison

"I am so sick and tired of these petty asses want-to-be models." Alison fingered ombre golden and black strands from her forehead. "If another one of those malnutrition, fake ass I'm your friend, get in my face bringing up my business, I swear…"

"You've been in this business long enough to know everybody isn't your friend and basically it comes down to every one for themselves. Just relax, do your job, and when the day is over you have me to come home to baby." She watched as Alan flipped the white bow tie over then back.

He was right. Just do the job. He was her love, the man, who captured her heart with a golden lasso a million times over. Her slender fingers circled the black curls resting on top of his head.

"Kiss me." Her lips full and puckered toward his bronze face. Heat rose between them.

"Alison."

"Yes." She continued to kiss him. "Ten years," she mumbled between wet kisses, "ten beautiful years. No one thought we would make it this far, considering we started out so young."

They were only eighteen and fresh out of high school. He had a scholarship to Jackson State to play football. Alison begged her parents to let her attend the university. They agreed as long as she helped with tuition.

If two jobs would help finance her education so be it. She could not bear the thought of being without Alan. Mature, kind, and the perfect gentleman, he had the height and complexion of a bronze statue. Accentuated, by thick eyebrows, his honey brown eyes glimmered. The soft curly textured hair complimented every curve of his chiseled face.

"Do you remember the struggle I went through to be with you?"

He laughed. "I do. You got a job at the grease pit to impress me and your parents. I love you for it."

"You're right, baby, that led to my big break." In the days of a smoke-filled, grease-laden floor restaurant, Alison wore a tight mid-riff tee-shirt and short shorts.

Soon after enduring insulting remarks, groped by burly hairy old men, a well-dressed man took a seat at one of the round faux marble tables. As she approached the table, he stood and extended a strong hand that gripped hers tightly.

"I'm Calvin Jones." One gold tooth appeared with a smile comforted by a neatly trimmed goatee. The man handed her a small white card.

Alison stood wide eyed and fingered strands of hair away from her face.

"Talent Scout-Ford Modeling Agency." Words mumbled from her mouth. She flipped the card between coffee colored fingers.

"I was in here a week ago, your beauty mesmerized me. The color of your eyes has an amber glow, which definitely compliments your complexion."

She felt her cheeks. They confirmed her thoughts, red and hot. "Mr. Jones, may I get you anything?"

"I'll take a root beer and cheeseburger."

"Be right back with that."

Alison moved along taking orders to nearby tables. She side stepped to let the bus boy remove plates that had half-eaten food left behind. She placed the cheeseburger and root beer in front of the customer.

"I didn't get your name." His smile made his square jaw more evident and dazzling white teeth could have blinded her.

"Alison. Alison Jackson."

"Well, Alison Jackson, I believe you have what it takes to be Ford's next super model. The beauty you exhibit, long slender legs that accentuate your thin frame, you have a natural look, smooth, caramel, unblemished skin. You're perfect."

She slapped her bare stomach. "Me, a model. I like the sound of that."

"Earth to Alison." Alan startled her.

"I'm sorry, honey, I had a flashback of how this all started." She wanted him deeply at that moment, to get her groove on. "Alan?"

"Yes."

"You know what I want to do?" She winked at him. "Come here and let me show you."

On the king-sized-bed adorned with a satin metallic silver comforter, he slid over to her. The goose down pillows encased in matching cases with the initial "P" on them. The pillow-top mattress made Alan's body relax onto hers. As he lay on top of her, his muscular thighs rubbed against Alison's slender legs. His strong hands caressed her shoulders. He rubbed his face alongside hers. She arched her back, exposing full and perky breasts through a sheer pink robe.

She lifted her left thigh and a full round bottom covered by black lace thong. Her voice low and soft said, "Take me."

He palmed her breasts. He maneuvered her thong off. She felt her husband like it was their first time.

"Alan, we're going to be late for our dinner reservations." She wiggled beneath him.

"Oh, baby," he groaned, "we can be a little late." His tongue traced the outer edge of her perfumed ear.

She loved her husband and nothing or anyone would change that.

***

The exquisite Italian eatery located in the finest section of Atlanta's famous Peach Street was always packed and tonight was no different. Alan strutted over to her door. With his back straight, left hand holding the black suit lapel, Alan was confidant. Opening the door, he took Alison by the arm and gently helped her out.

His black suit and off-white satiny shirt and tie made her black, diamond-trimmed, dress dazzle. The long slit to the side exposed Alison's thigh from the hip. The back crisscrossed and the front was high covered. She didn't feel like showing too much skin, she wanted to tease Alan a little. Her husband was not like most men, he didn't mind if she showed some skin. He told her men are visual creatures, they will look regardless. Did Alan have a green eye? She on the other hand did. Now, Alison didn't mind if women looked at her husband, but not gawking in his face every moment her back was turned or for that matter if it wasn't.

During their college years of dating, many girls flaunted themselves at Alan. One girl, Janice Newman, persisted until she and Alison had an altercation. Janice's philosophy was if he isn't married then he's all game.

Alison became tired of watching Janice parade in front of Alan with her double cellulite booty that oozed through the openings of daisy-duke shorts, which screamed for help. With full lips, Janice wore deep red lipstick, which emphasize them more.

One hazy hot Mississippi day, the football team had just finished practicing and Janice, scantily dressed, walked steadfast forcing each butt cheek to shake and jiggle. The guys were charmed. Alan came off the field, Janice grabbed his hand, not noticing Alison was close behind. Janice pulled Alan down to her and parted his lips with her tongue. Alison felt her blood boil through the trail of her veins. She ran, but the damp grass caught her. She looked up to see Janice's lips stretched ear to ear and Alan frowning.

Alan tried to explain that he didn't know what she was up to, but Janice insisted that she and Alan had been flirting heavily for weeks. Alison stood and tried to wipe the grass stains off her pink halter outfit. With trickles of laughter and finger pointing from bystanders, Alison had become angrier and punched Janice in her already inflated lips. She fell to the ground, while Alison's long legs stomped her. Alison felt that she was watching herself swinging and punching. The next thing she remembered she was sitting in the dean's office explaining through tears. Alison and Janice never exchanged words since that day and Alan never mentioned her name again.

***

They walked into the dimly lit Italian-themed restaurant where "Concerto for Violin" played softly in the background. Some people recognized both of them. Some just saw the new face of the Atlanta Falcons. No one rushed for autographs, which was why Alison chose the quaint restaurant known for its celebrity patrons, but also for fans minding their own business.

The host led them to a table located in the middle of the room where beautiful chandeliers dangled. The table setting was elegant—gold-ware, goblets trimmed in gold, heavy gold napkin rings, and gold-trimmed china plates. This was the most beautiful place Alison had eaten in and the best place for their anniversary dinner. They had so much to be thankful for. Their parents were still alive and they continued to grow in love with one another.

With red curly hair a petite server approached the Perrys with a big smile. "Are you ready to order or do you need more time?"

"Yes." Alison pointed to the menu, and various appetizers.

Alan spoke without looking away from the menu, choosing a salad. "Can we order our entrees now?"

"Of course," the curly hair woman answered. "What will you have?"

Both placed their orders gazing and snickering with each other like teenagers.

With a wave of her slender hand the server added, "Would you be interested in a bottle of Georgrafico Brunello di Montalcina, year

2000?" A Northern Italian dialect—Florence, maybe escaped from the woman.

"Yes, please." Alison smiled.

CHAPTER 2

Alan

Alison's dazzling brown eyes filled him with love. A lucky man he was to have her by his side. He loved her during high school. College, however proved to be a challenge, for both of them. Then he belonged to a group called Alpha Rules made up of football players. A rival group to the Wolf Pack-basketball players.

Drew Langston of the Wolf Pack had the hots for Alison and followed her around school every day. During their junior year, Alison decided to give Drew a chance. The dating went on for months with Drew pressuring Alison for sex. He promised her everything a college student could give, very little, but he tried. As Alan knew it, Drew would buy Alison a bunch of red carnations, bags of candy and once he offered to take her out for a fabulous dinner…at the grease pit she worked at. Alan would watch Drew snake around the halls wearing his basketball jersey scouring for Alison.

He waited and soon enough Alison realized that Drew wasn't the guy for her. That same Janice Newman that chased after Alan, was dating Drew. Alan was relieved that the light was finally shining and Alison would now be his—again.

"Hey," Alison said as she sipped on her wine.

"Yeah."

"You must have been in a daydream. You were staring a long time at your food."

"Oh, you won't believe what I was thinking about, but it's not a big deal."

Alison looked over her glass at him. "What?"

"Thinking about our college days, those were some crazy ones." He winked.

"You want to talk about it? Well, if you don't want to talk about it, we don't have to." She sipped more of the wine.

He reached for her hand. "Alison."

"Yeah, baby."

"Let's start a family."

Sliding her hand away from him, Alison, picked up her glass, sipped, and looked over the top. "Okay."

"Are you sure baby?" He asked.

"Yes."

Either it was louder than before or Alan didn't hear the rest of her response. "So, baby, that's it, yes?"

"What do you want me to say? I said yes."

"You don't seem too excited." Alan lowered his eyes.

"Next you'll say I should stay home and give up my career." Forcefully, she gulped down more wine.

He looked around hoping to not bring attention, "I didn't say anything about you giving up your career, but you would need to be home. That is something most mothers do for a while. I mean that's natural thing." His deep Southern twang drifted. "And I make enough money to support us, baby. It'll be all right."

She squinted. "Alan Perry, this is not about gender roles. I want a family too, one day, but that doesn't mean I have to stay home. So, here's the deal, you stay home with our child."

What just happened? One moment they were having a nice dinner and Alison changed. And what did she mean one day? They discussed this many times, but now he remembered Alison always slithered her way out of the conversation.

"We might as well end this conversation and dinner right now, Alan. You're not telling me what to do with my career. Yes, you may make more money, but with remarks you're making, you're lucky I'm still sitting here with you. Actually, I've lost my appetite. Since you make the money, take care of the bill. This was going to be my treat, but you can handle it, right, Mr. Money Man?"

She snatched her handbag from the table, pushed her chair out, causing the centerpiece to topple over. Before she walked away, she rolled her eyes at him. She turned with grace, allowing her slender frame to remain statuesque. Then she disappeared through the revolving door. Patrons at nearby tables hissed, whispered, and pointed. Frowns were upon Alan.

The server came back. "Do you want a container for this?"

"No, thank you, just the check." He forced a smile.

Outside, his steamed wife stood near their car, arms crossed. Through the deep side split of her dress a beautiful toned leg appeared. Alan stood directly behind her inhaling the intoxicating perfume. With the warm gentle breeze, the scent danced around his nostrils. Slowly, he opened the door and gently took her arm. She hesitated, but relaxed when their eyes met.

As he drove through downtown Atlanta, a mixture of jazz and r&b echoed. Alison loved to listen to both when she wanted to relax and he hoped it would work this time.

"I'm sorry, baby. I never meant to demand anything of you. If you want to start a family, I'm all for it. If you don't want to stop modeling, I'm for that as well, I'm sure we could work this out. I don't want us to be like this, especially on our anniversary."

Her eyelashes fluttered twice. "Alan, you can be such a pain. I forgive you, but you're going to make it up to me."

He smiled, knowing he had gotten over one hurdle, but more was to come. In a quiet area, behind a security gate, their driveway surrounded by well-manicured Red Maple trees on each side led to a sprawling home. Alan pulled into their four-car garage and parked next to his vintage 1967 Mustang Shelby. Alison's black Lexus sparkled.

The Cadillac Escalade was too bulky, but maybe it was best to keep if they wanted to expand their family.

Alan's suite jacket flapped as he danced over to get his waiting wife. When he opened the door to the kitchen, Alison playfully grabbed his butt. He turned to her, smiled, then gave her a peck on the forehead. He continued planting light kisses on her ears and neck. The butter-softness of her thighs as he caressed them gave his manhood an endless supply of blood. With his mouth open, he met hers. As he kissed her deeply, tongues playing circles, he cupped her butt and moved closer to her. She placed her arms tightly around his head.

Slowly, he unzipped and moved the dress down from her shoulders. Alan gently bit and sucked her neck. She moaned and twitched of the tickles. Finally, their lips met again. Somehow, he and Alison made their way to the kitchen island with its copper pots and pans that hung above and he lay her on the marble counter. He gazed upon her. Still looking at her, Alan removed her black three-inch heels. Her toenails elegantly painted black with silver swirls and a diamond on her first toe.

He removed his shirt and tie while she unzipped his pants. The black slacks fell from his waist. Stepping out of the expensive clothing, he took off his shoes and socks. Alison sat up and he pulled the dress over her head. His hand traveled south until it reached her place of enjoyment. "Baby, you're so ready." Soon after his lips traveled the same direction.

"Alan…"

"Yeah…" he kissed her, "yeah, baby."

This time her voice was a few octaves higher. "Alan…"

He winked. "Alison, are you okay?"

"Yes. Stop. Don't you want…um?" she tried to continue, "don't you want me to repay you the same?"

"No, baby, not tonight. I want you to enjoy everything."

While Alan continued to pleasure his wife, he glanced up. She was drenched and her eyes rolled back. Her legs shook and tightened with each trick he played. He hadn't even begun to make love to her yet. Her body shivered and jerked. He gently lay his 230 pounds of muscle onto her and pleased his wife. Their bodies moved in sync. An orgasmic shock traveled through Alan's body, causing an uncontrollable jerking motion. Forgetting the pots and pans hanging above, his head banged into them.

"Damn it."

"Are you okay, baby?"

"The question is are you okay?" Alan rubbed his head.

"Perfect, baby. I'm perfect."

"Mrs. Alison Perry, I love you."

"I love you too, Mr. Alan Perry. With all my heart I do. Happy anniversary."

CHAPTER 3

Alison

"Alan, it's early, where are you going? Come get back in bed with me," she said, rubbing her eyes.

"I thought I mentioned to you last night I had to meet with the coaches. You know I'll be starting practice soon and they want me to be familiar with how they do things here in Atlanta."

"Ah, baby, it's our anniversary weekend. Will you be gone all day? I still have some fire left in me." She pulled the covers back to reveal a caramel naked body.

"I don't know, Alison, but I'll be sure to get back as soon as I can. Make sure that fire doesn't go out." He kissed her on the forehead, grabbed the keys to the Escalade, and rushed down the spiral stairs.

Alison jumped out of bed, slid into her silk white robe, and stood next to the oversized picture window. Overlooking the circular driveway, she watched her husband closely as he backed the enormous truck slowly out of the garage and accelerated in the direction of the security gate. She let her toes sink into the plush white carpet as she sat on the pale blue European foot stool.

Their home 14,156 square feet, stone abode, had nine bathrooms, five bedrooms, a two-story foyer with floating spiral staircase, a two-story great room, family room, and home office. Each room had its unique kind of décor.

The family room was equipped with two arcade-styled games, a sixty-four-inch, high-definition flat-screen tv with a surround sound bar and each corner of the room surround speakers were mounted. A soft creamed-colored carpet accented the brown leather sofa and oversized dual leather chairs that sat centered in the room. Diagonally from the tv sat a pool table and a rack on the wall held six cue sticks. An old-fashion popcorn maker completed the room.

Alison was startled when the phone rang. "Hello."

"Hey, baby girl, how are you?"

She cleared her throat. "Tim, is that you?"

"Yes, it's me."

What a surprise, Alison hadn't heard from him in four years. They met when she was in New York for a photo shoot. "How did you get my number?"

"Your mom. I called to find you. I miss you, Alison."

"I miss you too. I just can't believe I'm talking to you."

"How's the married life?"

"Wonderful. Alan wants a baby."

"Oh."

"So where are you, Tim? Still living in New York?"

"Yes. You know I can't leave this town, too much excitement. So, where's that husband of yours?"

"At a meeting. He's getting ready for practice with the Falcons."

"Since he's gone let me keep you company?"

"Boy, stop it, how are you going to get here so fast?" She really did miss him. They had each other's back though Alan didn't accept him at first. He thought Tim was like every other man trying to get in Alison's panties.

"Tim, what are you doing now? Are you still an executive for Promo USA?"

"Yeah, sweetie. I like the money, it's darn good and the benefits are the best."

Alison heard somberness in his sultry voice. "What's wrong, Tim?"

"Felicia and I broke off the engagement. I'm missing her that's all."

"What…Felicia, the Jamaican girl?"

"Um huh."

Alison had made her way into the living room where a white sofa and love seat were. Pictures sat in crystal frames that glimmered with the sun rays. Vases and French miniatures decorated a white and pink marble sofa table. Her toes dug into the deep plush pale pink carpet. "What happened." She sat on the sofa crossing her legs.

"She had an affair and she was into that voodoo stuff. You know I don't get down like that. Every time she got mad at me…she threatened to use it. Shit, at times I was afraid to open my mouth and say anything to her. It got to the point if I didn't fuck her right, she'll voodoo me up." He laughed and continued, "But for some reason I miss the crazy girl."

"Humph, you miss her and don't know why?" Alison laughed. "Tim you had what…five or six years with her?"

"Something like that."

"Naturally, feelings evolved and it wasn't all bad with her, right? Besides, when you're talking marriage with someone it's serious. So, it can be very painful to end it."

"I guess you're right, Alison. It should've been you in my life. When are you going to divorce Alan and give me a chance?" He laughed, but Alison knew he was serious.

"What did I tell you about that? Don't you let Alan hear you talking like that. You know he always figured you just wanted to get me in bed. Also, I'm not divorcing my husband, we took vows and I plan to adhere to them."

"Okay, I won't say it anymore. I don't want to offend you or lose your friendship. The truth is, I love you. You know that. I don't want this to be our last conversation until the next four years or so."

"Tim, I love you too. I promise I'll keep in touch. Can I reach you at this number?" Alison wiped a tear away, glad to hear from a true friend. She hadn't made any friends in Atlanta yet. As she wrote down the number to later program, Alison heard a male voice in Tim's background.

"Who is that, Tim?"

"No one, Alison, but I have to go and I'll be in touch, okay, sweetie?"

"You take care and I'll make sure to tell Alan you called."

***

Already 9:30 a.m. Alison hadn't eaten and didn't know what she was going to do until Alan came home. She could go shopping at one of Atlanta's popular shopping arena, the Underground, but it was just too hot out to be bothered. Atlanta's weather was beyond hot. When the meteorologist said it was going to be eighty degrees, he really meant ninety. After she dumped the chemicals of a perm, flat ironing was time consuming for her thick long locks, but better, she wasn't going to sweat out a perfectly straight hair style to dip in and out of stores.

After showering, she slipped on a pair of purple silk pajamas and slippers. She decided to make a relaxing day of it. The sun beamed through the kitchen skylight, and shone against the marble counter, the counter that was used as a temporary love nest. She stood with arms wrapped around herself, looked at the shining pots that Alan bumped his head into. Taking one, she filled a medium amount of water into it.

The stainless-steel tri-door refrigerator had all the junk and healthy food she and Alan could eat. She took one egg and milk from the right side of the fridge. Boiled eggs were becoming a thing for her. Alison also discovered toasted multi-grain bread tasted delicious with honey sweet butter. She gulped down a tall ice-cold glass of milk that refreshed her throat.

After breakfast, she retired to the family room and popped a Blu-ray disc in. She opted for a Denzel Washington movie. Any movie with him was good enough for her. Not only was he a great actor, but handsome. He was her fantasy husband. Alan hated when she referred to him as that.

Alison hadn't noticed the changing weather, but the sky had become dark with swirling gray clouds and gusty winds. A loud thunderous boom followed by heavy rain startled her. The fierce high-gusting winds blew rain into the windows with strong force. Hail the size of golf balls pounded the pavement. Was a tornado near? Just as she flicked the light out in the room, Alan walked in looking like a submerged chocolate bar.

"Hey, baby. You want something to eat?" she said, handing him a nearby towel.

He wrapped his arms around her waist. "No. I had lunch." He wiped his face and arms, "I missed you, baby." He kissed her lips.

"I missed you too. So, what do you want to do? Doesn't look like we have a choice on outdoor activity."

"I want to relax with you. Holding you close to me is fine. Can we go cuddle in bed and watch tv?" Alan continued holding her.

She laughed. "I just watched a movie, but we probably can catch something on satellite."

"Anything is fine as long as I'm with you."

Alison took his hand and led him slowly behind her up the spiral staircase. He slapped her on the behind.

"What is your problem?" She said and ran the rest of the way.

By the time she made it to the bedroom door Alan had caught up with her. Grabbing her gently, he tossed her onto the king-sized bed. He removed his wet clothing. Alison down to the bare none sat back. How would she please her husband?

Alan moved slowly toward the bed. Alison aggressively pushed him down so she could take position. Her tongue played tricks around his ears and trailed to his neck. She squeezed his muscular arms and gently bit his nipples. She found his erogenous zone and licked and sucked until her mouth was full of him. With her free hand, she stroked him fast. When he was ready, she took her place on top. Anything to satisfy her husband. Her love.

"Alan, guess who called?"

He shrugged. "Don't know." He nudged her cheek with his nose.

"Tim."

Alan's brow crinkled then he spoke. "Timothy Jackson?"

"Yes. It was good to hear from him. He and Felicia broke up."

He laughed. "I guess he called to let you know in case you're a free woman. You know, if you had married him, you wouldn't had to change your last name."

"I told you, Tim and I are just good friends, stop joking. He told me about Felicia because that's what friends do, share the good and bad."

"I know, Alison. I like Tim, believe it or not."

This surprised her. Alan never expressed his likes or dislikes too much. How would he feel about her next statement?

"Honey, we should visit Tim, both of us. It would be great to get away before your season starts."

"Alison? Do you want to go visit Tim?"

"I do, but if it's going to be a problem then no."

"It's not a problem. Why would you think that?" He held her tighter.

"I figured you wouldn't feel comfortable with your wife crossing states to visit a friend, a male friend that is."

"I trust you and I like Tim. He has been there for you, the both of us matter of fact. When that photographer tried to rape you and I wasn't around to protect my baby, Tim stood up to the plate."

Alison tried to wipe that horrible time out of her mind. She was in New York on a photo shoot and a manly, oversized, grotesque woman came on to her. She was the best freelance photographer that Ford had at the time, but it was Alison's first time working with her. Alone in the studio, she asked Alison to open her shirt a little so she could get the natural her. As the man-woman with small prickly facial hair positioned Alison on the layout, her hands continuously roamed and touched the exposed breast. Alison couldn't help it, but in a way, it was turning her on. The want-to-be man whispered to her to relax and take a deep breath. Alison felt fingers gently squeeze her nipple. She squirmed and pushed the rough hands away.

The photographer stepped back and looked at Alison with curiosity. "What's wrong, don't you like it?"

"No." She gestured with her head while quickly buttoning the cotton shirt.

"Yes, you do. Don't be afraid. I can make you feel good, trust me."

"Please, Diane, I don't do this sort of stuff."

"Oh, baby," she said, reaching out to Alison in a comforting manner. "I don't want to hurt you or make you uncomfortable, I'm sorry."

For a moment Alison believed her. She was sympathetic. She hugged her and continued to whisper she was sorry. Then Diane started licking her earlobes and caressing her thigh.

Diane pushed Alison on the white pillows and lay her hefty body on top of her. Alison's screams were muffled by Diane's bear-sized hand. The man trapped in a woman's body had eyes fierce as a raging bull. With muffled screams Alison wiggled beneath her assailant trying to escape the foul breath and rough hands that continued to massage her between her legs. Tears flowed.

As Diane tried to accomplish her task, Tim walked in. Total amazement then anger, he grabbed the nearest chair and rammed it against Diane's head. The bitch slumped over with a loud thud to the floor. As she rubbed her head, she told Tim, Alison wanted it and led her on.

"No, I didn't, Tim." Alison's eyes filled with more tears.

"That little sleazy whore led me on." Diane continued to rub the now swelling bump.

Weighed down by disgust and shame, she buried her head into her hands and let the tears fall. She pulled her knees up and wrapped her arms around then rocked. Tim was cursing Diane with all the devil words. His eyes narrowed with a stint of red colored them. His hands now took the form of a ball. His breathing was rapid.

Diane quickly gathered her equipment and left.

Tim knelt beside Alison and allowed her to fall into his strong arms. "It's all right, Alison. We'll report this. It's a good thing I was early for our lunch date."

She sniffled and wiped tears that smeared her mascara. "Yes, it sure was good that you got here when you did. You know I didn't lead her on, don't you?"

"Of course, I know you didn't."

"I heard rumors about her from the other girls, but I didn't think she was that stupid to try something right here on the premises. I guess none of them pressed charges because she's still here, but this ends today."

***

A tear rolled down her cheek. "Alan, you know what I was thinking about don't you."

"I can imagine since we were talking about Tim. You must have thought about the last time you were in New York and that incident happened."

"Yes, I was. I couldn't imagine what would've happened with Diane."

"I was angry that I wasn't there for you, but it turned out good with Tim being there. I appreciate that so much."

"So, you really don't mind me going to visit Tim?"

"Baby, I love and trust you. If we don't have trust what do we have?"

"Alan, I love you."

CHAPTER 4

Tim

Monday morning, Tim stepped out the shower with a towel wrapped around his waist when the phone rang.

"Good morning, Tim. Were you sleeping?"

"Alison? What's up, baby? Is everything all right? Did Alan get angry because I called?"

"No. Nothing like that. Actually, I'm calling to let you know I'll be there soon."

"Are you kidding me? Are you coming up here for real?

"I am. Alan says he doesn't mind."

Tim was fully alert now. "When?"

"A week or so from now. Will you have time for me then?"

"Always, baby, always." Tim sang into the phone.

"I'm going to stay at the closet hotel near you. I was thinking—"

"Alison, you're staying with me. I have more than enough room. It'll give us more of an opportunity to catch up." With the pause he could tell she was uncomfortable with the idea. "If you want to that is."

"I guess. You know what, yes, I will. Two old friends getting together to share laughs and the good times."

"Thanks, sweetie. I have to get ready for work. Call me later when you're boarding the plane."

"Tim, I can't wait to see you. All those muscles…let me touch them, oh, I have to stop talking like this…. I'm just so happy that we'll see each other soon."

"Okay. See you soon." He listened to the quiet, wondering what it would be like to hear a woman's laughter in the brownstone apartment again. He needed Alison more than she knew.

***

The traffic in New York was frenzied. People hurried like busy bees. Shoulder to shoulder they filled the sidewalks. Some looked down at their phones or iPods. Rudeness filled the summer air. Tim raised an arm, waved, but failed to hail a taxi right away. Several passed him by. Finally, one with a shabby old guy slowed to the curb. The guy's hair was cotton-ball white with huge curls everywhere. He wore thick-rimmed glasses, and a wooden pipe hung from his mouth. Was Santa Claus here in the middle of summer? Tim laughed.

"Buddy, where to?" the deep, but gentle voice said.

"Thirty-Fourth Street, the Prudential building."

Tim sat back and gazed at the mass of people who filled the streets. He couldn't tell if the person was a man or woman who stood near a coffee shop with a tin cup in one hand and a sign in the other that read: *give anything a penny a nickel whatever you could spare. I haven't eaten in days.* His heart poured out to the helpless individual. He couldn't look very long for his own success made him guilt ridden.

As the yellow and black taxi swerved from lane to lane, Tim was thrown from each side of the smoked-filled box. The Christmas character looked in the rearview mirror and laughed. Up ahead was the tall mirrored building, Tim's place of financial security for eight years, the Prudential building, the most diverse place of people and many wonderful growth opportunities. He worked his way up from a mailroom clerk to Information Technologist. Actually, his buddy helped him along the way.

Drew was one of those boys from the South, but had a lot of city in him. He came to New York after a stint at Florida's A & M, hoping to land a job.

Tim and Drew met during an orientation session at Promo USA. Both worked sorting and delivering inter-office mail, copying files, filing, and shipment of products. With his good looks, charm, and a dose of persistence, Drew landed in the company's training and development program and with his bachelor degree in hand, he applied for and got the IT position. That's when Tim took a firm stand in his future and did the same.

He smiled, remembering how they became friends. Utilizing a full-size gym in the massive business building, Monday was hoop night,

Drew's favorite past time. They would take a time out, pace the court for a while, and talk about the days event.

"Hey, man!" Tim yelled.

Drew dribbled the ball down court. "What's up?"

"Don't be a show off, just shoot the damn ball." Tim prepared himself for a little dance.

"When I hit that net this game is over. You ain't got nothing on me, dude." Drew laughed.

"Talk shit all you like. Let's see what you got!" Tim yelled.

The ball danced between Drew's legs. Tim's gaze locked in.

"Boo-ya." Drew's hands rested in the air as the ball floated from a three-point mark.

"All right you played a good game this time. Man, where you learn to play like that? You have some structure, not street ball." Tim held his hand high.

"I played a little something back in the day." Drew tucked the ball under his arm.

Tim wiped sweat from his head and arms. "With skills like that you should've been on some body's NBA team."

"There was a time I wanted to. I was the guy in high-school and college. I mean look at me…" Drew cocked his head to one side. "I can play ball and look good, shit man, what female wouldn't want me?"

"Whatever happened to that girl you told me about. Someone you were so in love with?"

"Ah man, I had to let her go. She took up too much space in my heart. I needed to move on." Drew looked at the marks on the floor.

The taxi swerved, pulling Tim from his distant thoughts. He swiped his credit card in the payment box, jumped out, and breathed in the semi-fresh air. Before Tim knew it, he bid the cabby a melodious goodbye. He laughed at himself for doing such a childish thing, but the old man laughed as well. Tim enjoyed watching other people in high spirits, especially if he had anything to do with it.

***

"What's up, dude? You going to hold the elevator for me?"

"Drew. My man, what's up, dog?"

"You know, the same. Making love to my wife, hanging with the boys, and getting a little on the side."

Even though Drew claimed he loved his wife dearly, it didn't stop him from bedding every woman around town. He couldn't control it; he would say of his manhood. Tim didn't like the fact that Drew was messing around on his wife and once threatened that he would tell her.

That was the last time Tim joked with him, since Drew jacked him up against a wall in the men's bathroom and threatened to tell his secret.

"Oh, you went hanging out, but didn't call me? What kind of friend are you?" Tim honestly felt overlooked.

Drew eyes quickly looked over Tim, "I'm sorry, Tim. I figured you wouldn't want to be out like that. I was only having your interest at heart."

"You right, man. I didn't want to be out just yet." He looked over his shoulder and whispered, "talked to a friend of mines today and she really made me feel good."

"If she makes you feel that good then you should become more than friends." Drew chuckled while rubbing his chin.

"Naw, dog, she's married."

"So, what, she's married. A kiss and touch here or there won't hurt."

"Drew, how would you feel if some man was pushing up on your wife like that?"

Drew's head whipped around with narrow eyes, "My woman can handle herself. I know I give it to her good. I mean damn good and she has everything she needs—she won't stray."

"The question was—."

With a tone lower than before, Drew responded, "I know what the question was. All I'm saying, Janice is happy with me. She won't let some other man come with his weak game. How would I feel? I wouldn't like it, but at least I'll know she still has the looks to attract and I'll be damn if she has the guts to do something like that anyway."

Tim knew, Drew was right in his own way, but if he had a sweet lady in his life, she'd be treated as a queen. He wouldn't let no harm come to her. He would be like Babyface in that song about cooking his lady breakfast, dinner, getting her clothes from the cleaners, anything to show his appreciation of her.

"Look, man, let's not make this a bad Monday," Drew said extending his hand for a high-five.

"You're right, dog, we cool."

A turtle moved faster than the next few hours did. Drew and Tim had lunch at the newest restaurant that opened in the building. A mixture of Indian and Thai delicatessens. A weird combination, but whatever works for business. All the different restaurants on site were helpful for extreme cold or hot days. Just stroll from each eatery and have your choice.

Soon the five o'clock rush was on. People crowded the elevators, escalators, and even the stairwell; as if it were a Friday or upcoming holiday. Tim left Drew back in the office flirting with his secretary Mallory. She was fine with blonde wavy hair and ocean-blue eyes. Her lips were slightly full and her breasts stood at attention. No more than twenty-three, she looked like a mixture of a white and black barbie.

Tim climbed in the waiting taxi and dreaded the rough ride home. Exhausted, his body needed more rest. He leaned onto the passenger door with head supported by his elbow and closed his eyes.

"Hey, you." A man with a middle eastern accent gruffed. "Wake up and get out of my taxi."

"What the?" Tim mumbled between cracks of vision.

"Pay for your fare and get out," the dark hairy faced foreigner said.

Damn New York people just rude. Tim hadn't realized he drifted to sleep. The drool stain on his shirt sleeve was enough to convince him. He swiped his credit card and stepped out slowly. His legs were numb and breath was short. He fell to the ground, eyes gazed at the birds.

***

Bright lights blurred his vision. His body was heavy and ached. Tim was afraid he hadn't confessed his sins and now the good Lord had taken him away.

A heavenly figure dressed in white stood beside. "Mr. Jackson, you awake. We thought you would never wake up," the middle-aged woman said with a smile.

"Where am I? Am I dead?"

"You're at Lutheran General hospital. You've been asleep for a couple of hours. Your friend over there has been waiting." The nurse pointed to a sleeping Drew. She continued, "By all means you're not dead. You need some rest."

He raised slightly to see Drew asleep in the lounge chair. Tim's body ached; his mouth dry. He needed water. He reached over for the cup of ice, but dropped it due to weakness in his hands. At the sound of cold chips hitting the floor, Drew jumped from the over-sized chair.

"Tim." His voice was groggy. "Are you okay?"

"Yeah man, I'm fine. I'm sorry you've been here waiting for me."

"Just to let you know I'm not a punk, but you scared me, man. I wasn't far behind in another taxi. I wanted to tell you about my secretary and when I got to your building, I saw people standing around. I could hear the ambulance approaching."

Tim tried to be his amusing self. "Then what?"

"Then what? Dude, my heart started pounding. I saw you lying on the ground totally out of it. I didn't know what to do. I literally jumped from the taxi, pushed people out of my way, and knelt by your side."

"I didn't know you cared so much, Drew."

"I don't. I can't lose my only alibi," he said, bending over laughing. "But seriously, Tim, you're my boy, I do have a heart man."

Drew cared; he just had a funny way of showing it at times. The doctors came in, gave Tim the routine speech of taking his medications and staying fit. He heard this before so much he didn't want to relive it. He would sit with Felicia at her appointments and when her condition worsened, Tim was by her side twenty-four seven. At times he hated her for not knowing that she could've been affected.

She became sick often and lost much weight. Finally, the doctors diagnosed her with Chronic HIV, which led her into AIDS. She admitted to having an affair, not once, but twice. Tim's first reaction was to kill her before the disease would. He often thought how could she do this to him...to them? They were planning a wedding.

Many nights were sleepless. Many days were obscured with thoughts of their dwindling time together. Tim forgave her, but the damage was done. Now, he would wait to see where his fate lies. They sought counseling and began to pray together until the time of her death. By then they were at peace with the walking death. Felicia wanted Tim to make sure he was tested often and if the test was positive, she begged him to be strong and do as the doctors said. The one woman he loved dearly was taken from him as a thief in the night comes.

He didn't cry at her memorial, but smiled because he knew he would see her strong lovely face again. Drew was the only friend he shared the truth of her death with. For other friends and his family, Tim simply said, "She was a private person when it came to her personal life. I respect that and will you respect that as well."

Shortly after Felicia passed away, Tim's symptoms surfaced, and he kept his promise and sought medical treatment right away.

"Drew, tell me about this barbie doll you talking to."

Drew tugged at his shirt collar. "She gave me the digits. What else can I say?"

He was good at winning over the ladies. Two words and he could have their panties in his mouth. Drew needed to clean up his act. His wife was beautiful and Drew had a good career. He didn't need drama happening. As Tim heard from some of the other guys Janice wasn't an angel all the time. They had seen her in rare form when she thought Drew was out with another woman, which he probably was and had a good lie waiting.

"Are you going to take her out, Mallory, that is?"

"You know it and get some too."

"Drew, you said we're close, so don't get an attitude, but be careful, man. If Janice finds out what you have been doing all hell will break loose. Maybe you should just leave Mallory alone."

"I will, but not any time soon. Janice won't find out. My game is too tight."

Tim suspected that all Drew's romancing and whoring around had something to do with that lost love he wouldn't talk about. He was trying to fill a void.

"Thanks for being here with me, you're really the only family I have. With my parents deceased and my evil stepsister, plotting her net takeover of our parent's small fortune, I'm glad you're here, man."

"I'm glad I'm here too. So, you haven't heard from that sis of yours?"

Tim adjusted the blanket. "No. She'll call when she thinks something is due to her."

"Okay, Tim, I better get going, so you can get some rest. Hey, why don't you take the rest of the week off and make sure you get plenty of rest."

"The rest of the week that's too long besides I'm taking off next week, when my girl comes to visit."

"Oh, that's right, your friend." Drew rubbed his chin. "Make sure I have a chance to meet her." A half smile appeared.

"Yeah, right. Get out of here and kiss Janice for me."

"Later, dude."

Tim wasn't about to let Drew meet Alison. She wasn't about to become one of his game pieces.

CHAPTER 5

Drew

As Drew sat in the glassy black Lexus his thoughts carried him away. This was going to be an evening, have dinner with my wife, and maybe get a quick love session. I loved Janice, but I just don't feel fulfilled. She's wicked in bed, car, or wherever we decide to do it, but my heart wants more or does it want someone else? I never wanted to hear or think her name again, but this is getting to be awful. I have a habit ever since college. That day, I tried to convince Alison that I really did love her and was sorry for cheating on her. She dissed me and then her wimp for a boyfriend, Alan, tried to confront me. It's his fault that my career didn't go the way it should've. Now, he's living the life with her that I should have been able to give her.

At first, I followed her every move from Mississippi to New Orleans, then I decided to let it go. Alison is a beautiful and talented lady. She's the only woman who can stop my doggish ways. I know she is.

Alison never forgave me for dating Janice behind her back. She hated me so much; she flaunted her curvaceous body and flirted to get a rise out of me. Which she did. She always has and always will have that torch to turn me on.

The toot of a car horn brought him back to the present. As he drove, he noticed the new One World Trade Center. Reminiscing of those planes crashing into the World Trade Towers one by one and seeing a ball of flame, Drew shed tears.

At his Manhattan home, he could smell the aroma floating through the air. Janice was a good homemaker, though it was after nine p.m. She made sure Drew would have something hot to eat. He had called from the office to let her know he would be home soon and make him a sandwich. She was physically fit. Round and tight butt attached to well-toned legs. Her arms had a slight definition that fell beside firm breasts.

"What smells good in there?" He sniffed toward the kitchen.

Janice twirled, letting the kimono robe dance open. She greeted him with deep and wet kisses and view no man could resist. "Baked beans, greens, macaroni and cheese, and meatloaf. You know this isn't good to eat so late, Drew."

He hugged her tightly. "I know, but, baby, I'm hungry and it does smell good. Besides, you didn't have to cook all this. A sandwich would've been fine." He never wants to lose her, despite his womanizing ways.

"Honey, you work so much and never have time for my hearty meals anymore. I want you to be happy and satisfied." She turned her neck to the side, encouraging him to kiss it again.

"I'm sorry, baby," he nibbled on her ear, "I will make more time for us. I promise."

"Sit down and eat, I'll be in the bedroom if you need me." Janice planted a kiss on Drew's forehead and quietly left. She turned on the intercom and soft jazz music echoed throughout the Victorian-styled home.

When he finished the delicious meal, Drew carefully put the dishes in the dishwasher and went to the upper floor. He heard the jacuzzi whirling and Janice clinking glasses. As he approached the master bath, Drew peeked between the French doors and saw Janice laid back against the jacuzzi with eyes closed holding a glass of wine. He quietly walked in taking a strawberry from a nearby wired stand, dipped it in whipped cream, and placed it lightly on Janice's lips. As his wife nibbled on the delicate fruit, he gently removed his clothes and stepped into the warm bubbling water. Slowly, he moved in between her legs until their lips met. As he kissed her and licked the remnants of whipped cream, he began to wonder about Alison. With each kiss his thoughts of Alison became intense, thoughts he fought to remain buried. Drew guided himself into Janice and pulled her gently toward him. He took in the sweet scent of her perfumed body and felt the softness her skin gave while he exploded within her. In his mind it was Alison he saw and felt, but when Janice called his name, reality returned.

"Drew, where were you just now?" She squinted.

"I was here. Right here with you, baby." A sluggish smile as Drew pulled her close.

"You were, hmm. That was different."

Drew knew the way he pulled and kissed her as the way he would do with Alison and no one else. "What was different?"

"This little sex thing. Just different. I can't explain it really just different."

"Baby, with you every love session will be different."

After another two rounds it was well after two a.m. and Janice was the only woman on Drew's mind.

***

"Good morning, Drew." Mallory slyly smiled. "Did you have a nice evening?"

"Not as nice if it had been with you." Drew whispered.

She was so perky and vibrant he wanted to see just how much fizz she had. If they got together, it had to be on the down low. Drew figured Mallory was a little naive, and he could talk his way between her legs, but he wanted her to make a move for a date.

"Mallory, as you know, Tim will not be in the rest of the week, so all his calls and paperwork will go to me. Sorry, I don't have too much time to chat right now."

"Oh, okay, Drew. Go ahead I don't want to be a bother."

Damn, that wasn't what she was supposed to say. He wanted her to make a move. He wanted to get in those panties. Was she playing with him? Maybe that was her way of foreplay. Calm down, he thought. The day will come.

He went into his large office, with twin leather guest chairs stationed at the desk. He looked to the right, where the long rectangle silver tone clock hung and right below a tiny shelf with a picture of him playing basketball in college. To the left was cherry oak cabinets with double doors that enclosed a medium sized TV, Blur-ray player, and iPad often used for training.

The picture window gave him an aerial view of New York City. Sitting in the soft leather high-backed chair he glanced at his cherry oak desk. It had a glass cover over it, which he put pictures of Janice and him underneath. His theory was while he worked, he could have a view of them together and tame his wandering ways. Lately, however, it became boredom. Drew fought the feeling every day to remove those pictures. He didn't know why he felt that way, but again, he loved his wife. Unfinished business with Alison maybe.

His marriage would be over pronto if Janice found out he still had deep and loving feelings for Alison. Janice probably felt that she had won the battle since she got him, but when he went back to Alison to express his deepest feelings and apologize, that put insecurity in Janice.

She would always question Drew throughout their time in college. She wanted to know who was going to be at the basketball practices and where he was going afterward. Once she asked Drew if he still loved Alison. He couldn't lie. He thought telling the truth was the best thing to do…then. When Drew told her that he did love Alison, but not the way he used to, that didn't matter to Janice. After that confession Janice searched Drew's room until she found a picture of Alison with her number on back. As any typical and insecure woman, Janice called Alison and gave her some nasty new names. Drew wasn't proud of what Janice had done. Despite his admission of truth, she had no right to call Alison.

Drew gripped the edge of his desk as he thought more about how he lost Alison. His anger grew more toward Janice and the need to hurt her overwhelmed him. His thoughts replayed that final night over and over.

Alison and Alan called Drew and cursed him thoroughly. He heard the tremble in Alison's voice of pure hurt and hatred. His heart had dropped even more. She told him that she wanted to be friends and thought it was working in some odd way, but after the stunt he pulled she never wanted to see or talk to him again.

Alan had offered his unwanted two cents in as well. "Drew you ain't shit. Though, I don't approve of Alison continuing to talk to you, she's a responsible and mature girl, so, I trust her to do what's right. If that means remaining to be friends with you."

Drew didn't know telling Janice that he still loved Alison would've caused all this. After a few more obscenities shared with Alan, Drew sat and looked out the framed square bedroom window, trying to gather what happened.

Days went by when he saw Alison in school, she would cry. Drew had to know what was so terrible about what he said.

"Alison, baby, what's wrong? What did I do?" He gently took her hands.

"Let go of me. She snatched away. "How can you touch me after what you said about me?"

"All I said was I still love you."

"Sure, you did. Men always trying to talk their way out of something."

"What…is it so wrong to still love you?" He reached for her again.

She stepped back. "It's not wrong if you didn't think the person was a slut, sucked your nasty ass thing, that you only wanted to screw and pass me along to the rest of the Wolf Pack."

His eyes widened and then narrowed. "I didn't say any of that. Where are you getting this from? Did you hear this from some loser?"

Through tears, Alison laughed. "I guess that is what girls are when they are with you?"

"Who?" Drew was treading angry every minute of who he thought it was now.

Tears fell faster. "Janice. The night she called me…" Alison sniffed. "she told me how you hated me for ending our relationship and you were just being a friend to me because I was having issues with Alan, which isn't true. Then she told me to stay away from you and stop trying to come between the two of you."

Janice had played devil's advocate. She didn't believe that Drew loved her and was being faithful to her. Her insecurity caused him to lose the friendship of someone special.

After he apologized to Alison, for Janice's lies, he searched high and low for Janice. When he found her, she stood against a locker with arms crossed and blew pink bubbles from her gum. As he approached, she took one last chew and said, "That bitch won't be bothering us anymore."

He wanted to slap her filthy mouth. Instead he told her it was over, no explanation, just over. She knew what was up because from that day on she apologized for her behavior and constantly begged Drew to take her back. After a few failed relationships and seeing Janice in a mature woman's body he decided maybe they could put the past behind them.

Alison had never forgiven Drew for that day. This chain of events wouldn't have happened, had he not cheated on her.

A light knock at Drew's door woke him from the past. "Come in."

"Sorry to bother you." Mallory spoke softly as she closed the door. "I wanted you to have this." She dropped a neatly hand-written note on the desk and gracefully walked out.

He opened it, noticing a beautiful scent floated in the air. He inhaled it for a few seconds and read.

I'm sorry Drew if I appeared to have been non-chalant about your comment. I didn't want to give any indication that I'm flirting with my boss. I did notice that you were asking to see me later. We can meet at Champs Sports Bar around six p.m. I would love to get to know you better, unprofessionally. She signed it with a winking emoji.

Mallory came through! Drew knew she had the hots for him. Mallory was good to look at with pouty, but full lips, wide hips, tiny waist, and medium-sized apple-like breasts. Her skin was flawless and naturally tanned. She was beautiful. She wore a multi-colored silk peasant shirt and black nylon capris. Her sandals mirrored the shirt perfectly. Drew noticed the neatly French manicured fingers and toenails. Picture perfect she was. Her curly mane was twisted and pulled into a ponytail held by a clip. Oh, he was going to have a good time with her, better stock up on the condoms.

After Drew re-read the perfumed note, he noticed Mallory forgot to include the address and directions. He decided against emailing her, fear of their secret rendezvous being traced. He definitely was not texting her and leave a trace behind. Nothing. He buzzed Mallory to his office again, she glistened in the sunlight. He asked for the information, which she gladly recited.

Drew was on his way to the meeting place in a majority white neighborhood. Not that it mattered, blacks and whites didn't live in segregation any longer and most definitely there was more interracial loving than ever.

"Drew, over here." Mallory frantically waved.

"Mallory, hi." He wanted to appear professional. "What are you drinking?" He led them to a nearby table.

"My favorite, Smirnoff Ice. Try one?"

"I heard about that drink; guess I will try it." They sat at wooden square table that faced a large flat screen tv.

As he scoped the scene, he saw a few black people, and was relieved a little. A young woman smiled and placed their drinks on the table. He saw Mallory give a *he's mine* stare. The server smoothly, touched Drew's hand as she pushed the bottle closer to him.

"Hey, are you Tyson Beckford, the model?" Her smile turned to a glow.

That was the first time he was mistaken for a celebrity.

Before he could answer, Mallory butted in, "No, he's not and I appreciate if you would stop flirting with him thank you."

"Flirting? Honey, I'm a fan of Tyson and this fine young man resembles him a lot. All I wanted was an autograph if so. No disrespect intended." She walked away with a huff and let her green eyes stroll Mallory up and down.

"What was that all about, Mallory?" The first sign of possessiveness.

"I didn't tell you this, but you do resemble Tyson Beckford. You are fine. I guess I want you all to myself whenever the opportunity allows." Slowly her eyes closed and opened.

Drew found someone he possibly could spend a little time with and not become involved with. Nope, just a booty call on his terms. Yeah, that was a good idea. They talked about everything they could in three hours. After Mallory had her share of drinks, her ocean blue eyes were covered by droopy lids. Her slurred speech hinted that they get a hotel room.

As he paid the bill and escorted Mallory out, he turned and saw the semi-attractive server again and winked his eye. "I'll be back," he mouthed.

She smiled and winked back.

"Hey, Mallory, are you able to drive?" Drew helped her balance.

Standing upright, Mallory spoke. "I can drive and do whatever you want." She glided her tongue around her pouty peach-colored lips.

"You, miss, won't be driving right now. Come on get in."

Surrounded by thick trees and limited lighting, Drew parked in one of many available spaces.

He moved strands of golden locks from Mallory forehead and kissed. "I will get us a room. You stay put little lady."

"I'm not going anywhere."

Drew put his arm around Mallory's tiny waist visioning the softness of her naked body against his. "Room 10" they sang in unison. When he opened the door, they looked at each other and slowly stepped in.

He stood in the bathroom's doorway and watched Mallory across the bed on her back. When their eyes met, Drew winked and licked his lip. He unbuttoned his shirt as he walked toward his conquest. Deep rhythmic sounds echoed through his phone's speakers.

He pulled her from the bed. Golden tresses fell around her tanned face, highlighted by ocean blue eyes. Drew slowly rubbed her shoulders and nestled her head to his. For a moment they both inhaled slow breaths. Drew leaned into her and kissed deeply. She responded with a rhythm that matched.

Mallory pushed him onto the bed and unzipped his pants. He lay back with hot anticipation. She dove her head between Drew's legs and blew hot breaths through his pants. He slid his pants and underwear off. Mallory smiled. She gave him undeniable pleasure.

Drew couldn't contain himself as Mallory surprised him every second. His body lost control. Though a satisfaction would be glorious for him, at this point he wanted to see what else Mallory had in her.

Safe sex was always one of Drew's excuses that he could continue to do what he did. While he prepared, Mallory removed her blouse and capris. No panties. Hot diggity dog. He stood behind her, licked his forefinger, and gave her partial pleasure. While she squirmed and grabbed the crisp sheet, Drew pushed wildly into her. He lay on his back and positioned Mallory on top. "Ride'em, cowgirl, ride'em." His leg's tightened, back arched all while letting the sensation leave his body, as he gripped her tiny waist tightly.

After napping, they woke to another round of pleasure, this time for Mallory's satisfaction.

"Drew, you made me feel so good." Her voice light and sensual.

"Ditto."

"Oh, baby, we have to get together again and soon."

He wanted to get with her again, but not so soon after. He'd have to keep himself energized for Janice as well. She too was fantastic in bed. "We'll see, honey, I'll let you know when the time is right." He kissed her forehead.

"Don't keep me waiting, Drew, I don't want to hunt you down." Her mouth slightly crooked and half opened eyes, cautioned him.

"Drew?"

"What."

"I was only joking. You have to learn when I'm serious, but I can say this, you are a good love machine."

He stroked her hair. "I aim to please."

"I guess it's true…once you go black, you don't go back." She burst into laughter.

"Are you saying that this is your first time with a black man, Mallory?"

"Yeap."

"Are you serious? This first night you don't want to go back?" A chuckle slid from his mouth.

"Well, I'm not saying I would never. I just haven't been pleased this way before. You know any man can do the job; it's finding the right one."

"I understand. Hey, we better get going. I don't want Janice to start calling me."

"Hmm, um, do you love her?"

"Janice?"

"Yes, your wifey."

"Of course. She's my *wifey*." He mocked her.

"Why are you here with me?"

Damn, why women can't leave well enough alone. He didn't have time to answer Mallory's hidden, jealousy, and paranoid questions. He should've known most women were the same. Get with a man then start the game.

"Well, Drew?"

"Mallory, we talked about this at the bar. We both find each other attractive and intelligent. We did agree that we wanted to get in the sheets, right, and tightened each other up when needed."

"Yes…"

"So, if we agreed, Mallory, there's no reason for you to ask me 'why am I here with you.'"

Her eyes rolled upward.

"This will work baby." He placed gentle kisses on her breast and thighs.

CHAPTER 6

Alison

This would be the first time in years that Alison and Alan attended a church service. Time for them to get back into God's grace. When you have been separated from God, you can feel the pain. They were going to Mt. Zion, the prominent Missionary Baptist Church. The new building built across the street from the landmark church where Dr. King, Jr. preached a sermon. Alison remembered visiting the old church during a visit to ATL years before. She enjoyed sitting in the original pews and listening to a recorded sermon of Dr. King.

"Alan, are you ready?" She yelled while putting her watch on.

"I'm ready as ever." An ear to ear smile. "So, are we going to sit in the back of the church?"

"Why would we do that?" She poked him in the side, "we will sit in the front."

At 10:30 a.m. it was already a scorching day and she hoped it wouldn't get any hotter. She made her way into the SUV. "Alan put the air conditioning on." She huffed and patted her forehead with a handkerchief.

The church parking lot was full. Some of the women were dressed to impress. She couldn't believe some had on party attire. Is this what people thought of church, a fashion show? The Bible did say, 'come as you are', but they took it literally.

She and Alan walked past a group of people. Some stared, whispered, and pointed. She didn't mind, but today was not the day to be rushed for autographs or tons of questions.

One teenage girl, dressed very conservatively, approached the Perry's in a meek manner. Next to her was a little boy with the same style of dress, but his clothing was a little tattered. As the girl spoke, she never lifted her head. "Excuse me, ma'am. I know you're Alison Perry the model and that's your husband. May my little brother and I have your autographs?"

Alison didn't see any adults with the children. People started yelling at them to leave the Perrys alone. The pastor had just arrived and quickly approached the children.

"Quita and Marcus, you know how I feel about you or anyone in this congregation bothering these people."

"These people," Alison mumbled. "Pastor. The children were not bothering us. In fact, I would love for them to have the autographs only if Quita will hold her head up and look me in the eyes."

"Is this okay, Mrs. Perry?" Quita asked in humble voice.

"Yes, it is, Quita, and never hold your head down again. You are a beautiful young lady. Now let me give you that autograph."

As she signed her name Alan did the same for Marcus. Alison explained to the pastor that it was all right the children came to them. They didn't understand like adults do, besides adults got carried away. With that done and watching the children walk into the sanctuary, the Perrys found a seat three pews from the front.

Dressed in red and gold robes, MZC etched on the lapels, the choir led a song for devotion. Short, bald, and aging, a deacon came with a scripture and prayer. Everything was structured.

The pastor began his sermon, titled, The Sign of the Time, with his message flowing from the book of Revelations. He talked about various life-changing events including 911, Hurricane Katrina, and the War in Iraq. When he got down into his sermon, the congregation was all amen and halleluiah with the musicians playing right along, hitting a chord on the keyboard every time the pastor said amen. Before long it became a holy-ghost-filled sanctuary.

As the pastor neared the sermon's end, some people cried and hugged for comfort. When the invitation was given, Alison looked at her husband and he at her.

Extended were the deacon's hands for the Perrys or any person to come and stand before the congregation. She held Alan's arm tighter as they made the walk of life. After the pastor prayed and welcomed them as new members to his church, Alison hugged her husband and they followed the secretary to the office for more information.

After service, those members still around greeted and congratulated them. A short woman who looked to be thirty approached the Perrys with a pleasant attitude. She had a little girl who stood as pretty as a china doll, with a tiny rainbow dress and white sandals on. The child's hair had many soft curls and a rainbow headband held some in place.

"Hi, praise the Lord for you. My name is Tonya and this is my daughter Asia. Say hi, Asia."

An angelic voice whispered as she hid behind her mother. "Hi." She was adorable.

"Well, hello, Asia, my name is Alison and this is my husband Alan. You are a pretty little girl, how old are you?"

Still hiding behind her mom, the pretty princess spoke. "Four."

She introduced Alan to Tonya and they talked until reaching the parking lot.

"Here's my number." Tonya handed to Alison. "If you need anything, church information…" Tonya shook her head side to side, "I know it's all available on the website, but you know any odd questions or just want to talk."

Alison took the number and smiled. "Okay."

"Well, okay. You two have a great rest of the day." Tonya took Asia by hand, stumbled forward, looked back and waved.

"She seems to be really nice." Alan said.

"She does. I guess I'll have a friend in town now."

"I hope so, so you can get out more often other than your traveling."

"Alan Perry are you saying you're tired of me being around?" She playfully jabbed him.

"One day you should invite Tonya over for dinner so you girls can get to know each other."

"For the little time we talked, I know we have some tv shows in common and love to shop." She laughed.

"Well, honey, I want to spend some time with you before you leave for your trip to New York tomorrow.

"Sounds like a winner to me."

They drove casually along I270 with the mid-summer sun blinding their way. Alison exhaled when Alan rubbed her thigh through the white crochet dress. His hands, wide and strong, yet soft. She welcomed the feel. She loved him so much, she couldn't see them apart. She leaned over, laying her head on his shoulder. Both their parents had been married between thirty and forty years and the Perrys wanted to exceed that. Their relationship was strong and loving, but most of all filled with God's presence.

When they reached home, Alan told Alison to wait. She watched him slowly and gracefully come around to her side and open the door. When she finally stepped out the car, he leaned her against it and kissed her passionately. Alison felt his touch firmly on every inch of her body. She didn't know what had gotten into him, but she was glad. He licked her ear lobes and turned Alison around as he continued down her neck. With both hands-on Alison's hips, he maneuvered her against him and she felt his long hard attention.

"We didn't do it in every room of the house like promised. So, I want you right now and right here." His breath was warm on her ear.

Alison eyes bucked. "Here in the garage?"

"Yes, baby, right here, right now." His kisses were wet on her neck.

She guessed it would be safe to have a round or two.

While she was turned away from him, he lifted her white dress and slid the black thongs down. He unzipped his white trousers and let them fall to his feet. He unbuttoned his shirt and rolled up his cuffs. With her dress waist length, he slowly glided himself into Alison. Alan smacked her lightly on the butt and continued his rhythm. Using the car for support, Alison stretched over the hood. Soon they were in seventh heaven. Alison lay against the car and breathed rapidly while Alan squeezed her arms. She gasped for air lying under the many pounds of muscles. Alan realized he almost suffocated her. He quickly got up.

Damn, Alison, this just gets better and better. I love you, sweetheart."

I love you too."

"Alison." He led her through the kitchen. "I want to hold you baby, just hold you."

Although she was ready to have a quiet day with her husband, she needed to call Tim and confirm the arrangements for tomorrow.

"Alan, you go ahead and get comfortable, I need to call Tim about my flight information."

With a somber look then smile he trotted up the stairs.

It rang several times when the voicemail came on. With short beeps behind the greeting, she was finally able to leave a message:

Tim, hi, this is Alison. Where are you, dude? Anyway, I wanted to give you the confirmation for tomorrow. My plane United 702 arrives at JFK 12:30 pm. I hope you have something exciting planned for my stay. I can't wait to see you. Talk to you later, love you.

Turning around she was astounded to see Alan standing nearby. Why hadn't he made his presence known? He wasn't eaves dropping, or was he?

Her voice trembled. "Were you listening to my conversation?"

"No, Alison. I just come back when I heard you say you love him." His arms folded across his chest.

"Oh, that, baby it didn't mean the same as I tell you. I only meant it as a friendly love, nothing more." Her hand smoothly caressed his strong face.

"It feels awkward hearing my wife say that to another man, especially after we just made love."

Here they went again. She ran fingers over her straight her. He was trying to find an excuse why she shouldn't go on this trip. Would she be wrong to go? She hadn't seen Tim in years and it would be so great to spend time with him.

"Do you want me to go or not." Her eyes rolled.

"What's with the eye rolling—"

"I told you it didn't mean anything and you standing there with your arms all crossed with that puppy dog look on your face."

Alan stood erect, but shoulders slumped, "If I didn't want you to go, I would say it. I fucking told you how it made me feel."

"Oh, so now you're cursing at me."

"Alison." Alan moved sluggishly towards her. "I don't know what just happened here. Baby, I'm sorry for cursing at you, but seriously…" his hands reached to her.

Alison stepped back. She looked in the fridge. "Do you want something to eat"

"Are you ignoring me Alison"

"No. there's nothing to talk about. I told you it was nothing and leave it at that."

"I know what you said, but you snapped on me, in my opinion for no reason."

"Nope. I didn't, but if you feel that way, sorry." She moved containers back and forth. "Alan." She grabbed his arm. "I meant it. I'm sorry." She kissed his lips.

***

No words were spoken when Alison entered the bedroom. Alan lay on the bed with headphones and listened to music. In the master bathroom, Alison prepared for a quick sensual shower. With a new loofa she massaged apple-scented shower gel onto her skin. She closed her eyes and enjoyed the warm water that trickled down her body. She lifted her arms, letting the water hit all of her. She turned and held her head downward. The water ran smoothly over her neck and back. When done, Alison grabbed the white plush towel and pat dried her soaking body.

The apple lotion went on smooth and silky as she rubbed it over her arms and legs. The ceramic floor was cold. Alison tip-toed to the door. Still wrapped in the towel, she stood next to the bed watching Alan's head moved to beats. Her fingers traced his leg. He glanced at her then closed his eyes back. Her hand palmed the bulge and she firmly closed her hand.

"What the…" Alan sat up quickly.

"Baby, I'm sorry about earlier."

"Everything is all good Alison."

She let the towel fall. The coolness gave her nipples instant erection. She straddled him. She felt Alan's hands on her waist. She twirled on him. She leaned forward and kissed her husband.

"Alison. I love you baby."

"I love you too."

Their bodies intertwined through the night.

The morning was beautiful and Alison felt good as she woke in her husband's arms, energized from their break-of-dawn sexcapade.

Dressed and in route to the airport, Tim returned the call and confirmed her arrival information. As she kissed her husband, Alison felt uneasy. She guessed the haunting thoughts of the 911 tragedy had returned. No matter how many times she flew since then, the thought was always in the back of her mind.

Alan spoke. "Hey beautiful." He held her hand. "What are you thinking about?"

"Us. I was thinking about us. I don't want to lose you. You know things can happen and we can be taken from each other suddenly."

Alan turned the vehicle into airport parking garage. Up level one, passing rows of parked cars, he went up another level.

"I'm not going anywhere, Alison. I'm here to stay, you can count on that, baby."

With tears she trembled. "Of course, you're going to say that," she sniffed, "but God has his own plans. I want us to grow old together and –"

"And what, Alison?" Mouth partially opened and eyebrows down. Alan parked.

"I want us to die together." After that she cried as if she just received news.

"Oh, sweetie, listen to me." He hugged her. "A family that prays together stays together and I believe that covers everything."

Alan walked Alison as far as he was allowed by the airport rules. "Now get on that plane and try to have some fun, baby. Everything is going to be fine."

"Promise?" She wiped her eyes.

"I promise." He kissed her deeply.

CHAPTER 7

Tim

Tim had a glorious week planned for them. None of it included Drew. He didn't want Alison to get wrapped up with Drew. He shouldn't even be with Mallory, especially since she worked for them. If Alison and Drew happened to meet, she wouldn't be interested in him, not only because she was married, but a dog wasn't her type. Drew was his best friend, but wrong is wrong.

The passengers were coming off the plane like a swarm of bees. Tim saw a beautiful woman, skin looked as if was kissed by the sun. Adorned in a multi-colored fitted mini skirt it accented the woman's long legs. The pale blue peasant blouse matched her sandals that had a line of silver in them. The polish on her toenails mirrored the skirt and a glistening toe ring gave an elegant finish.

When he followed the legs upward, past the firm full chest, the pouty lips smiling at him, he looked into dazzling brown eyes.

"Alison."

Her hair hung down just below her shoulders, styled in a deep wavy patter. They stood for a moment looking at each other then embraced. He kissed her lightly on the cheek.

"Tim. You look good."

"It's good to see you also." He took her carry-on bag.

The two walked arms around waist resembling a happy couple. Standing at the baggage carousel Tim glimpsed at Alison sending a text.

"What you doing?"

"Oh, just letting Alan know I've landed. I'll call him later." She brushed back a few strands of hair.

He turned her towards him, "We're going to this quaint place for dinner. There is entertainment as well, karaoke. You sing?"

Now Alison's hands were on her hips. "I can do a little something." She shook her head. "Sounds like fun, can't wait to get there. What are we going to do in the meantime?"

"Well, when we get back to my apartment, I'll get you settled. Is there somewhere you want to go?"

"Let's sit back and catch up on old times. Then head out to dinner."

"Sounds good to me Alison."

At Tim's apartment, while he took her luggage out of the trunk, he noticed her on the cell phone. She smiled and gestured Tim to come, then handed him the phone. He listened to instructions Alan rambled to make sure his lovely wife was taken care of during her visit. Tim handed Alison the phone for her goodbyes. With a smack in the phone and her sweet I love you, she pressed the red X button and grabbed her carry-on bag.

"This apartment is big and beautiful. It's better than the one I saw when I first met you. I like your décor here. You really have taste for a man. Or did…"

She stopped in mid-sentence.

"I'm sorry Tim, I don't mean to continue mentioning her name. You guys really had a bad break up, huh?"

"Yes. I guess I'll tell you what happened over lunch. You want something to eat?"

"You know, I will have a small salad, no dressing, and a small unsweetened tea."

"Make yourself comfortable. Your room is the second on the right, across from the bathroom. I'll place the order."

"Thanks." She took her phone and proceeded down the hall.

Just as he was about to order the food, the phone rang. He picked up the receiver with annoyance in his voice.

"Yeah, who it is?"

"Is that how you answer the phone, man?"

"When I know it's you." Tim shuffled menus.

Drew knew Tim was picking up a friend from the airport and wanted to get the low down if there was any to give. Tim actually was interested in knowing what happened the other night with Mallory.

"How you been, Tim? How's your friend you picked up today. Are you getting the booty or what?" Sounds of howling a dog escaped him.

"It's not like that man. I told you she's married, happily that is. So, did you get with Mallory?"

"You mean freaky Mallory. That's between us, bro. She did some things I was even shocked at. Shoot the saying that once you go black you never go back." He laughed. I went white and may never go black again besides Janice."

Tears formed from Tim laughing so hard. "Did she do you and was it good?"

"What? Tim the innocent wants to know if she went down on me. Yes, and I lost my damn mind."

"I'm not innocent, Drew. I respect the woman I'm with. That playing around shit ain't nice. Then you know about the other STD's. Do I have to remind you of Felicia?"

"I get the point, but man Mallory is good. She wants to see me again."

"Do you want to see her? Outside of work that is."

"Sort of, but on my terms. I didn't want her to become this possessive, hunt-me-down type of woman. I told her she has to be patient and I will call her."

"What did she say?"

"Check this out, man, she hesitated and looked at me all weird and shit, but she said okay."

"Just be careful, man. Look I have to go; I'll call you later, out."

"Out."

Tim ordered a pizza, small Greek salad, and tea. When Alison finally emerge from the bedroom. Tim had an eighties cd playing, and the food arrived in thirty minutes as promised.

"It's about time you came out. What were you doing in there?" he asked.

"Organizing my clothes. Besides I heard you on the phone so I wanted to give you privacy."

"Oh, that was nobody. Just a guy I work with."

"It must have been a hell of a conversation because the way you were laughing…"

Tim stood straight and smiled, "Just a guy thing."

"Tell me about Felicia." Alison stated as she reached for the salad.

He had forgotten they were supposed to have that conversation. Tim didn't know how to tell her he was HIV positive.

Alison sat on the hardwood floor up to a circular wood table. Tim followed, placing his drink and pizza down.

"So, what gives Tim?" Alison picked olives out of her salad. She sat slumped over with her legs crossed, like a kid.

"Felicia and I began having problems a few years ago and things spiraled out of control. I guess when you're hurting in your relationship you turn to whoever is waiting."

"You or her slept with somebody else?" Alison sat up now, fully at attention.

"Felicia did. She told me it was with more than one. We argued about that and money."

With a mouthful of salad, Alison spoke. "You're telling me you didn't even try to have an affair?"

"No, I didn't. I loved her?"

"You are the most respectful man I know. You and Felicia had something wonderful. Couldn't you have tried to work it out?"

"We did try. But the damage was done. In the end she wanted to go back home.

"To Jamaica. Just like that?" Alison swallowed her tea.

"Just like that." Tears fell.

Alison came and sat next to him and wiped his face. He put his arms around her and lay his head on her shoulders.

"It's okay, Tim. This hurt won't last forever especially when you meet someone else to take your mind off her."

"It's not that simple. I don't want to meet anyone else. Even if I do, my heart will always belong to her."

"Wow." Her eyes fluttered. "Such a good man."

It felt good to have Alison there. Maybe she was right if and when he met someone else it would bring love back into his life. But meeting someone would mean disclosing his situation. That was something he wasn't ready to do. He wasn't a scholar on the disease until it affected him. Now, he could write a book on it.

***

At seven-thirty Tim and Alison left the apartment. The restaurant was only a block away on Forty Seventh Street and still shoulder to shoulder of people on the sidewalk.

At the restaurant they sat at a table near the small karaoke stage. Alison ordered Shrimp cocktail and water. Tim, however had the half-rack of baby back ribs lathered in a sweet and spicy sauce.

On the stage they were entertained by a stand-up comic.

"I've seen this guy before." Tim licked his fingers.

They ordered margaritas on the rocks. Alison had two, breaking her diet rule of no alcoholic beverage. She smoothed the wrinkles from her outfit and walked patiently to the DJ. She took the microphone and look directly at Tim instead of the monitor.

She spoke softly. "I want to dedicate this song to my very good friend sitting over there. Girls, you see him, the handsome guy in the corner."

Most of the women looked Tim's way and let out some oohs and ahhs. As the music began, Tim's attention was fully on Alison. She swayed her head back and forth to the r&b beat. He recognized the song as soon as Alison let out the first beautiful note. The late Aaliyah's, "I Care 4 U." The words were touching as Tim listened to them roll off Alison's tongue.

Hey my baby you looking so down, look like you need some loving. Maybe you need a girl like me around…hey baby tell me why you cry? Here take my hand and wipe those tears from your eyes.

Some girls in the bar jumped on stage with Alison and started doing the background chorus with her. Then Alison came in full and strong again.

Can I talk to you? Comfort you? Let you know I care for you. Hey there sexy baby, why your girl leave you in pain?

The girls started wailing out the chorus again. Alison sang the song perfectly.

Hold on, stay strong, press on for me. I care for you.

She sang with so much passion. Men who were in awe after Alison's performance hit Tim on the back. Some gave high-fives. One guy told him he was a lucky man to have a friend like that and winked. Tim only smiled. He guessed some people didn't recognize her with the dim lights and her toned-down look from the glamorous pages.

Alison's skin was flawless and smooth. She didn't need the magic of make up like most women.

"So how did you like it? She whirled around. "I know I didn't sound too good."

"I loved it! Are you crazy? You sound good. I mean damn good. I didn't know you could sing." He embraced her.

"I can't. I just play around."

"Your playing around is good."

"Glad you like it then. I wanted to see you smile and I succeeded." She walked her fingers up his chest.

They sat in the restaurant for another hour ordered more drinks and talked with strangers.

One of the women who did background singing headed towards their table, swaying with consumption of alcohol and stopped dead center of Alison. "Hey, you're that model, right?" She stood with her hands on her hips.

Alison looked up with a half-smile, but answered, "Yes."

The woman squinted and replied, "You're married to Alan Perry, right?"

"Why do you ask?" Alison's brows crinkled.

With a flip of her hand the nameless woman leaned towards Alison, "Listen, bitch, how can you be out here with some other man when you have that fine-ass football player…"

Alison stood. "You need to back up…"

Tim stood in between the women. "Come on Alison we can go. This isn't worth it."

"No. I got this." Alison hand bounced back and forth. "She must think I am a bitch, but hoe I will whoop your ass, don't get this twisted."

The woman stood her ground, not breaking the gaze.

"Not that I owe you an explanation, but this right here…" she circled the space with her hands. "Is my business. My husband trusts me and vice versa. Maybe you don't understand that, seeing that you're here alone without a man." Alison's lips tightened and her eyes became smaller.

"I guess you famous people think you can do what you want. Your husband may trust you, but I bet he gets his freak on while you're away. He's a man, he's going to do that regardless of how attractive his woman is. You, on the other hand, should uphold your respect and not be out with other men. Society doesn't accept women cheating. Its basically a given for a man."

"Thank you for the advice, miss…"

"No need to thank me, but if I was where your husband is right now, I'll screw him good because I don't have a man, remember."

"You know what skank-hoe, you ain't worth my time, boo-boo. Trot on and be annoying to someone else, bitch." Alison sat down and kept eyes on the woman.

Tim continued to stand as the woman hurriedly walked away.

"Are you okay?" He asked.

"I'm fine. I was having a good time until that stupid-ass bitch came over. Why do people always act so ignorant?"

Tim haven't seen that side of Alison. "Don't let it bother you. You're here on vacation and we won't let anyone spoil this for us."

"Tim."

"Yeah."

"What do you think about what she said, as far as men cheating, it's in their nature?"

Tim wanted to be honest, but that might open up another whole can of worms. "We, as men, are visual creatures. Looking at a beautiful woman does entice our thoughts, even watching X-rated movies turn us on. I believe it would for anybody that is normal. Anyway, as far as cheating, it does happen a lot. Some men say it's just part of the game, to conquer as many women as possible, but for others temptation pulls them down. They're weak."

"You're not weak, unless you're putting up a front."

When she said that Tim confessed. "Alison, I love you as my friend, but part of my heart wants more with you." She sat motionless while he continued, "You're beautiful on the inside as well the out. Yes, I'm always flirting, but I restrain myself every moment not to act on my feelings. I know your marriage means a lot to you and I respect that. I know we can't do anything about it. I just hope you don't' see me different now."

She laughed, and then held his hand. I'm glad you said it first. I'm attracted to you too. I have had some very nasty thoughts slithering through my mind." She looked down. "But then I remember my vows. I understand you can be attracted to someone, but that doesn't mean you have to cheat. Besides what would we do after, if we acted on our desires?"

"I don't know, want to try it." Their eyes locked onto each other.

She sighed. "No, but we could go over there and take a picture together. Let's take two, so we'll both have one. Take yours to work and put it on the desk."

"Sounds like a winner, but you have to autograph it."

The night went on with more talking and laughing. Alison was the best company Tim had since Felicia.

Back at Tim's apartment, he had a night cap and listened to Alison chatter on.

"Alan wants a baby."

Tim looked at Alison, his night cap, and back at Alison. "Really? You don't sound excited." He swallowed.

"I have to think about it. I mean we talked about it many times and I never agreed to it."

"So, what was the talk about then?"

"He would say how it would make our family complete." She put her legs in a sitting yoga position. "I'm not ready for all that, I mean the baby stuff." She twirled a few strands of hair.

Tim gulped down the remaining liquid. "Alison, really, you been with this guy for a long time and things are going great for you guys right?" He kept his head forward and looked from his side vision.

"Things are good. At times I want a baby and others I don't. Can't explain it. I never gave him a for sure answer so he should know."

"That's not communicating—"

"Oh, I communicate with him. He doesn't listen." She stood.

He met her stance. "Look." He rubbed her shoulders. "All I'm saying is think about it. Having a family won't affect you."

"Are you the one that will be taking time away from the spotlight?" She pulled away. "This is my life and I'm so sick of everyone telling me how to live it."

Tim hands went up. "Whoa, I'm not trying to tell you how to live your life. Why you getting so upset? You brought this up."

In what seemed like hours, a few minutes passed. Both had sat on the sofa. The quietness amplified the intermittent drip from the kitchen. Adjacent apartment doors sounded like they were being slammed. People's hushed voices in the hallway were now clear.

Alison wiped tears. "I don't know. I don't know anything right now." She sniffed.

"Hey, everything will be okay." He moved closer. "We can talk about this another time. Why don't you go take a shower and get some sleep. This was a long day."

With the back of her hand, Alison wiped her nose. "Thanks. I'm a basket case I know." She snickered."

Tim stood in the hallway and smelt the fragrance of Alison's shower gel seep under the bathroom door.

CHAPTER 8

Alan

Alison called Alan every night from New York. In a few days he was to lay eyes on his beautiful wife again. Tonight, after practice the guys were meeting to play pool and darts. After entering the Flowery Branch Training facility, Alan parked the large SUV, next to Daryl's tiny 911 Porsche. He got out, all smiles and grabbed his gear. Daryl stood near with his sunglasses on, and chatted on his cell phone. He was a single guy who had to date every girl who approached him.

Since Alan came to the Falcons, Daryl tried to hook him up with a few of them. Alan wasn't blind to so many beautiful women, but all he had to do was think of his gorgeous wife, his everything. He loved the idea when they strolled down the streets, men's eyes bulged, mouths gaped, and some would stop their conversation with the woman they were with.

"What's up, Alan? His big smile widened.

Alan and Daryl exchanged hellos with one hand shake and partial hug.

Alan said a few words in between. "Man, just waiting to get yo big ass on the field."

He knew he was not much of a match for Big D, who was 300 pounds and stood at six five, playing defensive end. Daryl slammed him in the back with his free hand. He made Alan feel right at home, since he came to Atlanta, helping find his way around the beautiful city, giving him the do's and don'ts of hanging around the team, and Daryl's personal favorite—how-to pick-up women.

"Hey, man!" Daryl yelled looking back at Alan. "Are you coming tonight?"

"Pool and darts. Yeah sounds like fun."

"Pool and darts?" Daryl laughed. "Oh, that's been changed. We're going to this hot new club. Lots of booty smacking and titty bumping all night long."

"I don't know, man. That's really not my crowd anymore."

"Are you worried about Alison? Just live a little." Daryl eyes and shoulders went up.

"No, I'm not worried about Alison. We are trying to get back into church and I want to do right…" Alan's eyes searched cracks in the ground.

"Okay man, I'll respect that. All I'm saying is a little party isn't going to hurt."

Maybe he was right. Just attending wasn't going to hurt. Besides, it would be nice to get out of the house. Alan stayed home since Alison had been gone and once, she got back they could have all the time together then. Yeah, Alan needed some time with the boys.

"I'm down, man, I'll be there tonight?"

"Good, glad you can make it." Daryl hit him on the back.

"Let's get on the field before coach has us doing laps and pushups."

They had a good workout. The scrimmage was powerful. Guys fit and ready, came to the field with a win attitude. Alan confirmed with Daryl that he'd be at the club. However, Alan fought with the wrenching feeling of going, knowing he'd have to fight off a lot of hoochies.

At home well after six p.m., he saw the indicator light on the answering machine was blinking. It had to be his baby. It would be another two days before she came home. There was one message.

"Hi, Alison, this is Tonya. I'm not sure when you'll be back from New York, but give me a call."

Tonya left her cell phone number and continued, "Tell Alan I said hello. Talk to you later."

Tonya? The one from church. Her five-six frame, short bob hair cut accented hazel eyes set on a round face. Freckles adorned her nose. She was gorgeous. Why wasn't she married to her daughter's father, or anyone for that matter? From what little Alison told him, it just didn't work out. Alan's thought slipped into a place it shouldn't with Tonya.

***

By the time he finished showering again and eating a light dinner it was well past nine p.m. He managed to call Alison. Listening to her sweet voice and fun she was having in New York made him miss her more. He was glad she went to visit Tim. Lately, he saw a change in Alison's mannerisms and temperament and a much needed mini-vacation would do her some good.

Before leaving he spritzed cologne his chest. Grabbed his keys and headed to the garage and the phone rang.

"Daryl, I'm on my way."

A light giggle, "I'm sorry this isn't Daryl, but if you want me to be I will."

His heart skipped a beat and his hand felt weak. "What's up, Tonya? Sorry, I thought you were my boy Daryl."

"That's okay. You mean Daryl McGee, your teammate?"

"Yeah, you know him?"

"Not personally. Only from watching the games." Her voice was soft and sexy. She had an aggressiveness in her tone, but oh so gently.

Alan lost track of time as they continued talking about football and videogames. She was a football junkie like him. She often played videogames with Asia. She offered Alan to a match with him in agreement.

"Tonya hold on for a sec."

Alan push the green light on his cell phone. "Daryl, I'm on my way."

"You still at home, aren't you?"

"Yes, I'll tell you about it later." He fidgeted with the cordless landline phone.

"Alright man, see you in a little." Daryl was gone.

"Tonya I'm sorry for making you hold, but I really have to go. The guys are waiting for me."

"No, problem. Go ahead and have fun with your friends. And Alan, for putting me on hold for so long you owe me a game."

He responded slowly, "Okay, when Alison gets back, we'll set up something so you and Asia can come over."

She paused before speaking. "Sure. When is Alison due back?"

"Friday."

"Guess I'll have to wait until then. In the meantime, Mr. Perry, enjoy your evening and have sweet dreams tonight."

When she hung up the phone, Alan stood in a daze trying to read between her lines. She was flirting in a mild way and he should steer clear. He slowly put the phone back on the cradle attached to the wall.

The night was clear and hot. Alan cruised on I285 in the Mustang Shelby. Music with intense beats bumped from the Bose speakers. Alan was in a good mood. He drove with windows down letting the hot air caress his face. When he exited off MLK Jr. Drive it was 11:15 p.m. Daryl was going to blow a gasket if hadn't already. Finally, approaching the club in Midtown that r&b singer, Keith Sweat, owned. Alan pulled up to the valet. Stepping out the vintage car, he flexed his collar and hand pressed his khakis on each leg.

The club was packed. The music great and Daryl was right…there were more women there than Alan had seen out at one given time. Tall and short, dark or light skinned, long or short hair, straight or wavy. Some were abnormally skinny or pleasantly plump. Then you had the in between which he admired. Outfits were definitely eye catching. One young lady had on white capris, which hugged her oversized bottom. Her large breasts were screaming to get out the mid-riff top, but her six pack was awesome. A tribal tattoo that circled her stomach was sexy as hell against her light complexion.

He moved on to the rear of the club where Daryl was having a conversation with a female.

"What's up, D?"

"It took you long enough to get here, punk. What were you doing calling your sweet wife again?"

"Naw man, her friend Tonya called and we had a small conversation."

"Her friend, you had a conversation?" Daryl laughed low. "Hmph."

"It's nothing, man. She was wondering when Alison was coming back so they can get together." Alan tried to convince himself that was the truth.

"Okay, Alan, if you say so. What does she look like?"

"She's fine. Maybe biracial." Alan shrugged his shoulders.

"Fuck, Alan, you haven't even got any of the punanny and you're whipped." Daryl sipped from a glass.

"What the hell Daryl. I'm not interested in her punanny." How could he be?

"Whatever you say. Daryl turned to the female. "Alan this is June. June, Alan Perry."

She extended her small hand and with a big grin, "Hi, Alan, it's good to meet you. Is it okay if I get an autograph?" She talked fast.

"Um, yea, what do you want me to write?"

She fanned herself. "To June my sweetheart, I'll always remember you and love you, forever yours, Alan."

Alan looked at Daryl and then to the female. He wasn't going to sign himself into some type of law suit. Instead he wrote 'June thanks for being my number one fan, Alan.'

"I guess I can settle for this." She took the paper and pen, turned to Daryl, and asked, "So are you guys coming to the hotel for the party?"

"Baby, I told you we would be there. Give me the address again and we'll meet you later."

June scribbled on a napkin and handed it to him. What party and what hotel? Alan wasn't looking forward to hanging out all night. Sometime he could smack Daryl in his fat face for making plans for him.

"Alan, don't look so stiff. It's just a party. Imagine this scene moving to another room that's all." Daryl grinned.

When June left, they chatted with more women that was in their space. One girl approached Alan showing all teeth, glanced at her girlfriends standing in a line with their arms folded across their chests and stopped directly in front of him. Before he knew it, she dropped to her knees and put her head between his legs. Rolling her head around she massaged his manhood. He couldn't help the excitement that was penetrating through his pants. What just happened?

As he exited through the crowd, Daryl was on his heels, badgering Alan to go back and let the hoochie finish her thing. It didn't feel right having another woman do what Alison did so well.

As they waited outside for their rides, Alan, ran his hands through the curls atop of his head. He had been with Alison so long he forgot what it felt like to be free and wild. Of course, he loved her, but men could slip and fall.

When they reached their destination, again valet parking was the best option. Alan joked with the small frail attendant. "Don't drive off with my baby, you won't be able to handle her." He laughed.

The next guy waited anxiously for Daryl to get out of the car, apparently so he could drive around the block or two in the clean, sporty Porsche. Alan and Daryl took their claim tickets and entered the Intercontinental-Buckhead Hotel.

Room 1011, Daryl knocked loudly. No answer. He tried the door handle and they were in.

"Alan, look at all this. Women, women, and more women."

"Yeah, sure a lot of them. Where are the men?"

"Why are you concerned with men? Man, this is Heaven on earth." Daryl frowned.

"I'm not concerned about men. Just wondering."

"You know what I think?" Daryl rubbed his chin. "I think this is some girl on girl action and we're the spoons to stir it up a little." He laughed.

That motor-mouth girl Daryl was chatting with at the club was being sexually pleased by two other women. She was thoroughly enjoying herself as they used all types of toys on her. Another woman lay on her back with legs upon shoulders of a muscular, broad-shoulder woman. The woman had a strap-on. The scene was insane. Women lay with their legs in butterfly positions while others took turns tasting different juices. Some formed a sixty-nine position and gyrating to the current hit single echoing through speakers.

"So, pretty boy angelic Alan, are you going to have some fun or what?" Daryl rubbed his hands together.

"I'll hang around for a little, but ain't nothing going down."

"Suit yourself, man, a brotha has to get his." Daryl flicked his shirt collar, turned towards June and walked away.

Alan found a chair in the corner of the huge room, sat down, watched Daryl caress June between her legs. Two other women rubbed him on his chest and legs. Daryl lay his head back and eyes rolled back.

A beautiful tanned Asian woman approached him, sipping on a Corona. She wore a pair of yoga pants and a fitted top. Her four-inch heels accented her legs. Her hair was shiny coal black and hung near her bottom.

"Drink?" she offered.

Alan took the bottle from her hand and sipped. She sat on the floor next to the chair and started caressing his legs gently. He didn't know why, but more beer he wanted. He reached for it and she gladly handed it to him. This time he took more swallows, with bigger gulps. After ten or fifteen minutes the room started to spin.

Only thing he remembered was Daryl waking him up hours later. Alan's khakis were off and his shirt open. The room was quiet, only a few women still there. That girl he was drinking with was gone. His head spun.

"Daryl…" His hand supported a weighted head. "What the hell happened?"

"Man, I don't remember much. I was with June and some other freaks and they were giving me drink after drink. The next thing, I'm here with you on the couch." He struggled to sit up with bulging eyes.

Alan quickly checked his wallet. Surprisingly, everything was still there, even the small amount of cash he had. This was so weird. Some freaks just wanted sex, no money? Then the word caught him…sex! Did he? He pulled his boxer briefs down looking for any signs of sexual pleasure. He couldn't tell. "Damn!" Alan said. He yanked his briefs and shorts up and fastened his shirt.

Alan looked at Daryl, his face buried in his hands. This was his fault. If he hadn't persuaded him to come out tonight and to this party, he wouldn't be in this mess.

"What's the matter with you?" Daryl called out.

"Me? I shouldn't be here, but hanging with you…"

"Oh, don't blame this on me. You're grown man and can make your own decisions. You probably liked what you got tonight anyway."

"Like? I don't even know what the hell I got. Damn, Alison is going to kill me!"

Alison? I know you're not thinking of telling her about this."

"Look, Daryl, this was wrong and I don't keep any secrets from my wife. We can talk about this."

"Listen at you. If something happened in this room she doesn't need to know. I mean you don't know if anything happened. We were ruffied and maybe we shouldn't have been here, but hey, man, it's not worth telling her. See, then you're going to have her wondering every time you go out what you are doing."

Daryl had a point because this type of scene wasn't going to happen anymore. He didn't need Alison down his back every time he went out. Hell, she was in New York, how did he really know what she was doing?

CHAPTER 9

Alison

Alison thoroughly enjoyed her week with Tim. They dined at New York's exquisite restaurants and Tim was a perfect gentleman. He didn't attempt to get between her legs, though most men would've planned it as part of the week's visit. Alison was a bit curious as to why she hadn't heard from Alan since Wednesday. Usually a daily 'I love you' or 'goodnight' would be all that was said, but nothing in the last few days.

"Hey, girl, are you finished packing in there yet? I have breakfast ready."

The aroma of buttermilk pancakes and maple sausages wavered in the air. "Yes, I'm done."

In the kitchen, the table setting was a page from a home magazine. White plates, frosted glasses that had a yellowish tint, bright green and yellow napkins were folded perfectly, and silverware that had an ancient look to it. Scrambled eggs were in a yellow dish next to a green bowl that held fresh sliced strawberries. Hash browns completed the meal.

Who would think a man could do this. In the center of the table a single daisy flower bathed in water.

"Do you like?" Tim smiled and led Alison to her seat.

"Yes, I love the entire setting. Where did you learn to cook and set a picture-perfect table?"

"Felicia. She was studying to be an interior decorator."

Alison nodded in approval. "Oh, I'm sorry, Tim, I didn't mean to—"

On the way to the airport Alison thought about Alan. She couldn't imagine losing him, a part of her. She could feel Tim's pain. She reached for his hand and gave him a smile.

From the parking lot to the security check point no words were exchanged. Hand in hand, the two smiled. Tim gently stood back and gazed upon Alison, staring deep into her eyes. He kissed her lightly on the lips. Alison did the only thing she could, say goodbye and precede through security.

***

As a drummer beats his drums, fierce rain pounded the airplane, which hovered over Atlanta until it was safe to land. Alison couldn't wait to get her carry-on luggage and find her handsome husband. Dressed in a throwback jersey, blue nylon shorts, Nike Airforce Ones, and tons of gold chains a man in front of Alison chatted continuously with a flight attendant about his bachelor pad. No wonder he was a bachelor. She said excuse me three times before the man decided to move. When he turned around and saw her in a hot pink halter top and a white denim mini skirt, his attention immediately turned from the flight attendant. He told Alison how much he enjoyed her pictures and dreamed of meeting her.

"Baby girl, look at you, you so fine. I can't believe I'm standing right here graced by your beauty."

"Excuse us." The rest of the passengers huffed.

The annoying man kept talking. "Yo, Alison, can I get them digits. Maybe we can hook-up or something, you know what I mean?"

"No, I don't know what you mean and I'm quite sure if you know who I am, you know that I'm married."

"Girl, I know all that, I ain't trying to take you away from your football-playing husband, I just want to spend a little time with. I know you ain't one of those stuck-up hoes that think she's too much for a simple guy like me." Alison tried to interrupt, but he kept going. "Dig this, I will show you all the finer things in life, work hard for you, show you what a real man is about."

Alison looked around for hidden cameras. Was she being punked? "Look, real man…I'm honored that you feel you can give me the world, but I'm not interested okay, may I get pass please?"

She made it to baggage claim and Alan stood near. Hands in pocket and half smile he didn't come to her.

"Hey, baby, I missed you." He planted a kiss on her lips.

"I missed you too, Alan, more ways than one." She secretly rubbed him. To her surprise he stepped back and tried to remove her hand. "Baby, why are you moving my hand?"

"We're in public that's all."

"And—"

"And...all I'm saying is we can wait until we get home, honey. That's it."

She didn't know what to think. They never had a problem with public display of affection.

They walked to the parking garage after getting Alison's luggage, not saying a word to each other, but in a close embrace. She was so hot, her panties felt like a hole had burned through. She planned what she was going to do to him. Finally, they made it to Alison's Lexus.

"Honey, are you all right?"

He fidgeted. "I'm fine, Alison, why do you ask?"

"I don't know, you seem a little nervous or something." She shook her head.

From the moment she touched him, he was different.

"Ah, baby, I'm fine really. I guess I'm going through a phase. Our first game, the pre-season game." He quirked.

"You don't have anything to worry about. You'll do fine and I know Daryl will be there by your side like a big brother. Besides, this isn't your first rodeo. Alison liked Daryl even though he was a lady's man, but always treated her with high respect and love.

"Before I forget your friend Tonya called for you. She wants to come by."

"Really? Well, I'm kind of tired and I'm looking forward to spending time with you this weekend.

Her visit to New York was good, but being back with Alan was even better. Comfort hit Alison as she walked through the door. She removed her sandals and her toes sank into the plush carpet. She plopped down on the sofa and lay her head back. Alan struggled with the luggage while Alison sat still.

She flinched when the phone rang. "I'll get it!" She skipped to the fireplace where above on the mantel piece sat a cordless unit. "Hello?"

"Hey, girl, what's up? I was wondering when you were coming back."

Why didn't the girl wait until she returned the call? "Alan told me you called." Trying to sound as easy as she could Alison continued, "Tonya, I was going to call you later once I settled in."

"I don't mean to interrupt anything, but I just wanted to let you know that the Underground is having a big sale tomorrow and I'm taking Asia. Do you want to come along? We'll make it a girl's day."

"That sounds nice, but I was really looking forward to spending time with my husband."

"Finally, she said with disappointment, "Guess I'll see you Sunday then. That is if you guys are coming to church."

"Yes, we'll be there. See you then."

Alan finished putting the luggage away. His eyes were sullen, mouth drooped and his pace was slow. Alison had just what he needed to be pepped up. "Come here, baby, sit right here between my legs while I massage your shoulders."

He hesitated then sat down against the sofa, his back to Alison. She massaged around his broad shoulders, making her way to his neck. He sighed and breathed deeply. With the ball of her hand, she kneaded back and forth across the blades of his shoulders. She tilted his head back and kissed him softly on the forehead. He turned, positioned himself on his knees, his arms around her waist, he buried his head in her breasts. "Alison, I love you."

***

Sunday morning while they were having breakfast, Tonya called to confirm they were coming to worship. She was going to save them a seat next to her and Asia near the middle section in the sanctuary. Alison frowned.

"Alan, I'm not going today." She continued to eat.

"What. Why?"

Squinted eyes peered over the rim of her glass; Alan felt a knot in his stomach.

"I don't feel like going today, no reason. You go and be holy for both of us." She sat the glass down.

"Baby, did I say or do something?"

"For crying out loud Alan. Why do you think everything is about you? I said I didn't feel like going. You think you did something. Did you do something?" She shook her head and exhaled heavily.

Alan held tightly onto his plate. "You know Alison, I don't get you. One minute you're happy and the next you're upset. Whatever is going on with you, you need to take care of it."

She took another long and slow swallow of her juice. "Have a good day at church."

Sending its blistering rays, the noon day sun was in full effect. Across from the pool stretched out on a multi-colored lounge chair Alison sipped water with a lemon wedge dancing in it. The sun beamed. A light breeze floated between her toes, circled her face, and feathered her hair. How could he go ahead without her? Does he really think she was losing it? She continued to sip on the ice-cold infused water.

She jumped from the chair. Found music on her phone. She danced to the tunes, twirling and bopping her head. This is much better than going to church. A beep interrupted her tunes.

"Hey, baby." Alan spoke quietly.

"Hey. How was church? Are you on your way home?"

"Church…"

"What's wrong now Alan?"

"Church was nice baby. Sure, would've been better to have you there with me."

"I'm sorry. I didn't want to go."

"Alison, I have to ask you something. Did you stop taking your birth control pills?"

"What? Why would you ask me that?" She twirled a few strands of hair. "Yes, I did."

That was a lie. Alison wasn't going to stop. She didn't want children now or maybe never. She felt some kind of way leading Alan on all these years. A person can change their mind.

CHAPTER 10

Drew

Janice, wake up. You're going to be late for your appointment. You know how your stylist is." Drew didn't understand why she had to have a hair appointment at seven a.m., yet she could never get up on time. She knew her stylist, James, don't play the late game. He'd take other clients in a heartbeat.

"I'm tired, baby, do I have to get up?" She pulled the comforter to her neck.

"If you want that mess on your head done, yes." When she didn't wrap her hair with a silk scarf at night, Lord God, give them all grace because she was the perfect example of a bad hair day. Janice's hair was very coarse and needed much maintenance to keep a pretty sleek look.

She could lie here all morning if she wanted, he had to get to work. He was excited because some time had passed since he'd seen Mallory. She's been on vacation. When he hired her, he told her she could keep her scheduled days.

"Janice, it's 6:30, I ain't telling you anymore. If you want to miss your appointment all together so be it."

"I rather miss my appointment doing something productive." She peeked over the comforter. "It's my day off, I want to play, rest, and play some more." She massaged Drew's thigh.

"Come on baby, I can't be late for work." Drew couldn't get a good picture of him and Janice doing the nasty right before he was about to see Mallory. He needed a clear conscience to see her.

"What do you mean come on?" Janice tossed the comforter back. "Many times, you have gone in late, just so you can get a quickie. What's up with that, Drew? You ain't touching me anymore so who is she?"

Drew almost pissed on himself. She never accused him of sleeping with anyone and the one time she does, she was right. "I ain't messing around with anybody." He glanced at her then away.

"Oh yeah, you mother. —"

"You better watch your mouth!" He pointed at her.

Pointing at herself, "Don't you tell *me* to watch my mouth. You need to watch who you're putting your wet, limp, noodle into." As she sat there, arms now folded she yelled, "I found a condom wrapper in your car!"

She was snooping in his stuff! But he was so stupid to leave that kind of evidence around. "There must be some kind of misunderstanding because I haven't slept with anyone, baby. That wrapper, I don't know how it got there.

She looked at Drew with her mouth tight, squinting, and arms still folded.

Drew had a one-time thing with Mallory in the back seat before she left on vacation. As they were in route to JFK, she touched him and said how much she wanted to mount him at that moment. He couldn't resist. Her massages were strong and long, which convinced Drew to pull into a dimly lit park. He remembered taking off the condom, placing it in the wrapper, and tossing it out the window. He knew he did. Or did he? At least she didn't say she found the condom itself because Janice would have had the sperm tested. Drew tried to remain calm and figure out a first-class lie.

"Honey, look. I don't know when I gave you reason not to trust me, but you are the only one I want and will ever need."

"Humph! That's a bold face lie and the truth ain't in you!"

"What are you talking about now?" He tried to distract her from the earlier topic.

"You still in love with Alison."

Drew didn't think Janice would ever say that name again. They moved on since the incident in college. He could never tell her that he was, indeed, still in love with Alison.

"Aren't' you, Drew?"

Now at seven a.m. he was definitely late for work. Time didn't stand still, not for a second.

"Am I what?" He wrestled with putting on a watch.

"Still in love with Alison?" Tears fell down her cheeks.

It took everything Drew had, to lie. "No, I am not. I've always cared for her, but I'm not in love with her. Do you know how longs it's been since Alison and I were together? Too many years and we both moved on. I love, you Janice, you're my number one."

Drew had to get out of there. Now was a good chance—she had lowered her arms and stopped crying. He only had to make her feel secure and that they were okay, but he was the one with a problem. That problem was totally getting over Alison. He needed to see and talk to her. The way their friendship ended had caused a void in his life. Some way he had to talk to her then maybe Drew could get on with his life with his wife the way it should be. Not womanizing and bedding every woman he thought would take his mind off Alison.

"Janice, I love you and, baby, I promise when I get in this evening, we can talk about whatever you like, but I really need to go. Call me later if you feel you still need to talk, but I have to get a move on it and so do you. Go get your hair done, boo." He kissed her.

The ride to work was terrible and Janice made sure of that. Now, Drew didn't have a single thought of Mallory, but he couldn't help thinking of Alison. When he finally made it to work, Drew tirelessly pushed the up button and waited for the elevator. On his work floor, a few secretaries lingered in and out of the break room carrying mugs, some with strings hanging over, sipping the hot beverage. He didn't see Mallory among the staff, which was good he wanted to avoid her for a while, so he could gather his thoughts. Drew exhaled when he didn't see her sitting at her desk and walked at high-speed, giving quick hellos. Just when he reached for the handle to his office door, Mallory popped up behind. Drew dropped his briefcase. When a dog is up to no good the slightest thing makes'em jumpy, he thought.

"Hi, Drew." Mallory quietly sang.

He pivoted while bending down to pick up the briefcase. "Good morning, Mallory. I see you're back. How was your vacation?"

"Good. It would've been better if you had come," she whispered.

"I'm glad you enjoyed yourself. Listen, I have a lot of work to do and hold my calls except for Janice of course—put her through."

Mallory's face turned a cherry red. "Sure, but can we talk?"

"Not now, Mallory. I really have a lot of work to do. Maybe later is that okay?"

"Yes, it can wait, but not for long."

He became tired of women wanting everything to be in the now.

"Are you okay, Drew, you seem a little annoyed?"

Damn, maybe he should've just ditched work and Janice for the day. "Mallory, I'm fine. Now, will you excuse me. One thing—will you ask Tim to come see me ASAP."

"I'll get him. He was down the hall showing off—"

"Mallory, just get him please…thank you." They stared at one another. Drew took a few moments again to gather his thoughts. He didn't intend on being blunt with Mallory, but his day was not getting any better.

While he waited, Drew, placed a manila folder with the words in black print, *Deadlines*, on the center of his desk. Looking through the drawer, he pulled out another folder that was red titled, *New Complaints*.

"Hey, man, what's up?" Tim reached for a high five.

"Nothing, man, just have some problems I need to talk about."

Tim took a seat in the leather chair smiling down at the pictures in his hand.

"Tim, I'm in a world of trouble with Janice."

Tim didn't look up.

"She found a condom wrapper in my car, dude, and I need to use you as my excuse. I can tell her you borrowed the car—"

"I'm not getting into this. Janice isn't going to shoot my head off. I told you to stop messing around with that white girl…" he pointed to the door, "or whoever it was."

"Fuck you, Tim. It wouldn't make a difference if Mallory was any other color, the point is she's a woman and I slipped up this time."

"You got that right—you slipped up." Tim kept his gaze glued to the pictures and it was starting to piss Drew off. He already had Janice on his back, and soon Mallory would be for whatever reason she wanted to talk.

"Take a look at my pictures, it might make you feel better. When you see this woman, you'll forget all about your troubles."

He let out a sigh, took the pictures, sat back in his chair to see they mystery friend of Tim.

He looked down at the first picture of Tim and some unknown people. But when he moved to the next one, he couldn't believe what he saw. He felt as though he stopped breathing. His chest was tight, mouth became dry, and his heart rate sped up.

"See, I told you, you'll forget about your problems."

Now leaning forward on the desk, Drew held the picture up high. "I can't believe you know her, Tim."

"Who wouldn't know her? She's a top model and married to that football player, Alan Perry."

Drew stood. Hands in his pockets. Hands now against his forehead. "I know that. My God, this is who was at your house for a week and you didn't tell me. How could you do this to me?" He pointed at himself.

"You have lost your mind. I don't have to tell you who's at my house besides I didn't see a need to."

"Alison," he mumbled under his breath. "Tim, this is Alison."

"Earth to Drew. I know it's Alison. I just said—"

"I know what you said, but this is *my* Alison. The girl I told you about from college."

Tim looked at the floor. He shook his head.

Drew sat back in the chair, holding the picture at every angle. He couldn't believe she was there. So close. But this had to be fate that they had someone in common. Someone who would help him talk to her.

"This is the same Alison you were in love with and your mind ain't been right since you split up?"

"Tim, I'm still in love with her. Can you believe that? We had a terrible misunderstanding and I feel bad for it all these years. I need a better closure with her. Wow, my love never stopped for Alison."

Pacing the floor, Tim laughed. "I don't believe this!"

"Look, man, you have to call her and let me talk to her."

"I don't think so."

"Why not?" Drew stared.

"Not a good idea. She's happily married and don't need you interfering."

"I'm not trying to get back with her, like I said I need to clear up some things."

With both hands on the desk, Tim, leaned forward. "Why now, Drew? I thought you had other problems?"

Drew knew it was fate. Alison was just a phone call away. All Tim had to do was make the call. Once Janice mentioned Alison's name, old feelings surfaced. Each day for years, he suppressed the anger and guilt. That day Alison wanted nothing else to do with him.

He slammed his fist on the desk. "You act like you want her to yourself."

"What the hell are you saying?"

Both stared.

"I know you want her as a matter of fact. Remember our conversations, you talked about your friend from Atlanta so much, I told you to screw her, but you only said, 'No, she's a friend', as if that would stop you."

"Bullshit, Drew, you got it wrong. Alison is fine as hell, intelligent, and yes, I am attracted to her, but I will not jeopardize my friendship by doing that."

"Sure, man, whatever. I can see it all over your face. That's why you didn't want to me to meet her—you thought I would smooth my way into her life and bed."

"You're full of it, Drew, and you need Jesus."

"I need Jesus? Really? Where was Jesus, when I was trying to fix things between Alison and me years ago? I have the opportunity to say I'm sorry and explain, but you won't help me. And where is Jesus while you're suffering from…"

As soon as the words slipped from Drew's mouth, he lowered his eyes. Time stood still.

Tim turned, "That was a low one, Drew, even for you. You want to talk to Alison; I'll see what I can do."

"I'm not trying to get back with her really."

Drew sensed Tim's, hesitance, but he'd do it. He was a pushover when it came to sympathy. Drew really needed his help, this time. Hearing Alison's voice would ease some of his pain.

"Tim…I'm sorry for what I said."

During Drew's lunch hour he sat in his office daydreaming of the day he'd talk to Alison. This was the break he needed to tell her what Janice did and how he's been paying for it all these years.

As his thoughts of Alison brought a slight grin, Mallory entered with straight-faced. She carried a brown paper bag. He didn't feel like eating lunch with her. How could she invite herself in?

"Drew, we need to talk. I thought you would've called me the day I got back?"

Here she went with this. He didn't tell her he would call so why did she assume? Drew told her at the hotel that first night that she couldn't get possessive, but women don't listen. They say ah hum, yeah, okay, and whatever else to make a man think they have an ounce of understanding. He was excited to see her, but Janice ruined that with her early morning rant. Maybe he should back off with Mallory. Especially since he has a chance to make it right with Alison. Actually, he was confused, excited, and scared at the same time.

"Mallory, right now isn't the time for this conversation. I agree we need to talk, but later."

The blueness of her eyes seemed to darken and eyelids lowered. "No, we need to talk now!" Her voice stern.

"Did you actually come in here to talk or eat your lunch?" He amused himself.

"This is for you." She placed the bag in front of him then sat back.

"I'm not hungry…"

"You will be after you see what it is."

He paused before reaching for the bag. Mallory fidgeted and maybe she was ready to kill his black ass for what he didn't know. He made all attempts to be with her and talk to her even late at night.

He opened the bag. Drew didn't take his eyes off the content. He didn't remove it, couldn't move, but had to know why she was showing him.

"What's this?" He staggered out the chair and stood.

"What does it look like?" Her eyes now wide. She smoothed back her curly golden locks.

"A pregnancy stick, kit, whatever?"

"Yes." Her voice now low.

He pushed the bag towards her. "Why are you showing me. I always used protection."

"Drew, it's yours and I know you used protection, but condoms aren't one hundred percent safe. You know that."

"You have lost your *fucking* rabbit mind! No, this is a mistake. You've been sleeping around—"

"This is your, baby. Wait until I have the DNA test."

Have it? She couldn't. She wouldn't. Damn, how did this day go from bad to good to hell and it wasn't over yet. If there was ever a God, he needed him now. Drew was successful, married, and didn't need this type of drama. He had to play this cool. He had to think. And think hard.

"Mallory, baby, I didn't mean to yell, but you have to know this is a total surprise. He rubbed his chin. "I don't think you're sleeping with anyone else." He moved closer to her, reached down, and stroked her lock of curls. "I'm wondering why this would happen to us? We're young, goal-orientated individuals and I know a baby isn't in that plan."

He wanted to sound as mature and career minded as possible. She took his hand and wiped the tears dripping down her cheeks.

"Drew, I love you."

She *what*? Okay this day wasn't going to get any better.

"I know it's been a short time, but I do love you. You been there for me and I can count on you. I know you would be a good father to our baby."

Our baby. This wasn't happening.

"Can't you see how a baby would be an obstacle right now? I'm not saying that it won't ever happen, but right now isn't the time."

She sat upright and tilted her head. "I see. You want me to get an abortion."

He felt weak in the knees. "Yes, baby, I do. It'll be best for us both right now."

"If that's what you want I will, only because I love you and I know you'll be there for me."

This was so easy. She agreed with no hesitation. Could he trust her? At this point Drew had to. He didn't want to give her any reason to be angry with him and changing her mind. Mallory told Drew she had to leave early for a doctor appointment, which at that point he didn't care. He really didn't want to look at her.

Quiet all the way, Drew and Tim rode the elevator down to the first level. Tim couldn't believe what Drew told him about Mallory and of course he gave him the "I told you so," speech. Drew wanted to get home and finish the conversation with Janice. His day couldn't get any worse.

Walking through the front door he expected Janice to be standing with one hand on her hip and head cocked to the side like any normal mad woman. Instead she was in the kitchen preparing dinner, which confused him. This morning she was ready to rip his head off now it seemed all was forgiven. "Thank you, God." Drew whispered through clasped hands.

"Drew, is that you, I'm in the kitchen. Want to come on back?"

He was hungry since his lunch was over whelmed with an unappetizing menu from Mallory. He made way to the oversized kitchen. He watched Janice scurrying around the kitchen she decorated. The backsplash and base of the window was decorated with red bricks. The rest of the kitchen was eggshell in color with red crown molding.

"Hey, honey, how was your day?" She turned with a smile, still stirring what smelled like spaghetti sauce.

"My day? The usual with mad clients and all." Drew couldn't look at her.

"Hmm, that's all?"

"Yeah, would there be anything else? Oh, baby, your hair looks good. I see you got James to do it after being late this morning." Drew smiled, hoping the fire was out.

"No, no, I was wondering, maybe I was a little hard on you this morning." Janice continued stirring the sauce.

"Baby, you weren't hard, you did what any wife would and should do." His shoulders inched up.

She finished stirring and gathered the best dishes they had.

Janice probably felt guilty and wanted to make up, which was what he needed right now.

"Drew, you want wine or juice?"

"I'll take wine baby."

"Good choice. Sit down I'll get everything." She moved about the kitchen getting wine glasses, Italian bread, and butter. The tossed salad already sat on the table, with the toppings in nearby containers. She spooned a big helping of spaghetti onto Drew's plate with the thick sweet, hot and spicy sauce filling the air. She had half the helping he did. She sat and eyes moved over Drew. They ate in silence, but he kept catching a glimpse of her looking at him.

After the meal, Janice served them both warm apple pie alamode. Drew's stomach was filled and screamed for him to lie down. He stood, rubbed his stomach, and slowly moved toward the woman who made him feel good when it came to a good meal and sex. He kissed her neck and wrapped his arms around her waist. Feeling her, he felt the stupidity of messing around with Mallory. He helped Janice clear the table. While he put the dishes in the dishwasher, he noticed a luggage bag sitting by the back door.

"Honey, why is that bag there?"

She didn't turn from what she was doing, but answered in a shallow tone, "That's for you." She sniffled.

With uncertainty in his voice, "For me, why?" Are *we* going somewhere?"

"No, *we* are not, but you are."

"Janice, what's going on, I—"

She turned and threw a plate, missing Drew by inches, "I'll tell you what's going…that condom wrapper in your car belong to you, you dirty bastard. I guess you didn't have time to use it."

His hands up. "I told you I don't know how it got there."

"Sure, you don't. Well, tell me this, when were you going to tell me about your baby?"

She couldn't know, there was no way, deny it, Drew, deny it. "I don't know what you're talking about and I thought…" A slap came from left field on Drew's cheek.

"Oh, you more stupid than I thought. Let's call your little girlfriend...Mallory is it? She showed me the doctor's report and knowing you as well as I do, it's your baby."

"Mallory?" His world began to spin. He couldn't concentrate. He was speechless.

"You know, Drew, I've known for a while now that you were having an affair with someone. She's not the first either I'm willing to bet. The late-night calls, sudden job emergencies, too much work, have to stay late, not hungry for dinner, but you managed to keep up your sexual appetite for me. How close am I?

"I don't know what to say, but—"

"But my black ass. You had the nerve to bring this home. But guess what? You're out of here tonight. I decided to make you that last damn good meal to show you what you're losing."

"Janice, wait!" The table shook as Drew slammed his fist down.

Waving her hand as to swat a fly Janice said, "Don't say my name. It didn't mean anything to you when you were busy screwing someone else. Get out my house!" Drew never seen her this angry before. He was hurt because he had hurt her. His sexual encounters had caught up with him and Drew felt like the ass of an ass.

"Drew, please leave now and tell that tramp not to come by my house ever again or she'll get a good ghetto Southern whippin'. She's lucky I don't come up there to the office." She pushed Drew as hard as she could in the chest and then struck him in the face again. Drew didn't know where he was going. He had never thought that he'd be asked to leave his home. He only hoped that giving Janice the space she asked for would mend the situation.

He drove the speed limit on 195, exited, and drove by the Hudson River. He sat there and looked to the sky for answers. The sun was nearly at set. The mixture of red and yellow hues hovered over the water. He took the cellphone from its cradle and began to dial the number that was all too familiar, but now felt like a passing memory. Janice didn't answer. How could she do this. She didn't give him a chance to explain. She just took the word of some hoochie. What happened to letting your spouse plead their side of the story?

Drew was crying and with each thought of Janice more tears. He truly loved her, but she should've given him a chance. Somehow, he had to make everything right, including firing Mallory. If she was indeed pregnant with his child and wasn't going to get rid of it, then she needs to be employed elsewhere. He didn't want the stress and gossip around the office. Why was this happening to him?

"Tim, something happened and I need to stay there for a few days."

Letting out a lengthy sigh Tim asked, "What happened?"

"Janice put me out."

"Ouch!"

"Yeah, man, and right now I'm sitting here near the Hudson River trying to figure out what just happened. I mean I know what happened, but why it did."

Tim was speechless for a minute or so, then sighing again, he spoke slowly. "Is this about Mallory?"

"Yes."

"Look, man, I was in the restaurant during lunch and some girl, I assumed a friend of Mallory, was talking to a real ghetto fabulous chic."

"And?" Drew was getting impatient by the second.

"I heard her say that 'Mallory was going to get even with the black guy'."

"Wow." Drew laid back into the seat more.

"Tell me what happened and why did Janice put you out. You said that you and Mallory was going to talk later."

Drew brought Tim up to speed about his last supper with Janice after Mallory made a visit to his home. Silence. He couldn't blame Tim for being quiet. Either he was saying to himself that was good for Drew or he was cursing Mallory in his mind. Sometimes your friends had your back no matter the circumstances.

"Why did Mallory go to your home?"

It slipped Drew's overwhelmed mind that he didn't tell Tim what happened when she came into his office. This was getting worse again.

Drew was tired of living through it, but if Mallory was really pregnant, he was going to live through it for the rest of his life.

"Mallory is pregnant and claims I'm the daddy." He got out the car and paced. With a tightly closed fist, Drew pounded the hood of his car. His anger had returned back to the scene at noon, Mallory happy and ready with a loaded gun.

"Drew, come on over and bring something to drink. This is going to be a long night."

He could count on Tim if nobody else. He was a good guy. "I'm on my way and thanks, man."

As soon as drew placed the miniature phone back in the cradle, it rang with one of the melodious tunes programmed. The caller-id said unknown. Usually he didn't answer calls such as that, but his gut was telling him he had to. "Hello?"

"Drew. Before you say anything, I'm sorry of what I did, I—"

"What do you *want*, Mallory?" The last I heard from you; you were going to have an abortion. Oh, but how you changed your mind within hours."

"Listen Drew, I can't abort this baby. You said wait until later, but I'm not sure I'll be able to get pregnant again. For years I have battled with endometriosis."

"What the hell is that?" He really didn't want to hear any explanations, but guessed he better listen to what the little trick had to say.

"Endometriosis occurs in approximately ten percent to fifteen percent of women between the ages of twenty-five and forty, most often in women who have never given birth. The exact cause of endometriosis is not known, but one theory is that the endometrial tissue in menstrual blood—"

Really. She was really going to give text-book line-by-line explanation.

"The tissue forms cysts, or pockets of blood, on the pelvic organs."

Silence.

"Drew, did you hear me?"

"I heard you. So, you're saying because of this *possible* sterilization you have, it gave you the right to go to my wife and tell her about us?"

"No, and I'm sorry for that."

"No, you're not. You're full of horse shit. You could've told me this when you were blabbing off earlier. Less I forget, what is it that you have to get even with me about, Mallory?"

She sucked in air. "I don't know what you're talking about."

Drew knew Mallory thought he was a fool. "I know you told your friend that you were getting even with me. Unless you have been sleeping with more black dudes."

"Grace wouldn't tell you that. Have you been interrogating my friends?"

He chuckled. "Grace? If there was nothing to tell where would the interrogation come in at? Just admit you ran your mouth off."

"No! Drew, I swear, I was just talking in anger. She's my closest friend and after you and I made our decision I talked to her. I needed a female perspective and—"

"And you ran to your big-ass friend who by the way was telling somebody else your…I mean *our* business."

"Drew—"

"Mallory the most that bothers me is you went to my wife. What are you hoping to accomplish by doing that? You want my marriage to end?"

"I was angry!' She sniffled.

"Angry. Look, Mallory, I don't want to discuss this right now and I'll appreciate if you stay away from my wife and me."

"We need to talk about our baby. You can't just walk out my life. You didn't have a problem fucking me! You're just like those black men that run away from their responsibility. No wonder a lot of black women are turning to white men for love and security."

"And yet you screwed one of those black men."

He never ran from his responsibilities nor was he planning on it now. He wanted time to process all that has happened, but she was being difficult. "I'm not going to let your angry comments destroy what little sanity I have at this moment. You can call me all the names you like, but remember this—you need me in that baby's life and you didn't have a problem giving this black man head. Goodnight, Mallory."

Drew hated to end the call like that, but Mallory had issues that he couldn't fix. At least not the way she wanted. He could be there for the baby and all, but her entire attitude seemed to have changed overnight. One minute she was this mature and beautiful woman he was attracted to, and then she was a psychopath out for revenge.

He parked in an unmarked spot across the street from Tim's building and completely forgot about drinks after talking to Mallory. He grabbed the bag that Janice packed and looked up to Tim's window in the brownstone building. He felt like a dog that wet on the carpet, chewed too many of the owner's expensive shoes, and humped every stray female dog around. Now he was being punished and kicked out of his doghouse. Quite honestly, he had only slept with two women, which included Mallory, since he'd been married. He was not the dog that Tim thought. Yes, Drew flirted heavily, but he didn't go around hopping in bed with every woman. A few people walked their Poodles,

Pugs and Terriers, while others jogged under the street lights that shone brightly. Drew admired the calmness and stepped into the quiet building.

When Tim opened the door, no words exchanged. Drew sat on the sofa. To his right, a picture of Tim and Alison hugged up on what looked like the ferry stared back at him. Tim didn't have that picture at the office and Drew could see why. They looked like a happy couple. Alison was dressed so sexy, a pink and white maxi sun dress. Her amber streaked hair glistened in the sunlight. Tim's muscular arms held around her waist.

Drew blurted, "I need to talk to Alison as soon as possible."

"Aren't you enough trouble as it is?"

"I need to talk to her. I have to set things straight. I really need to do this Tim."

"Let me think about it, man."

"Don't think too long." Drew leaned in. "You can be right here and make the call for me. Explain to her that you two have a mutual friend and I really need to talk to her. Tell her I made you call." He clasped his hands.

Tim laughed while putting the glass of orange juice down. He grabbed his cell phone.

"I'll call, but this is going to go down in history."

When Drew heard him speaking to her, his heart beat faster. His hands were slippery from the sweat and shook.

"Are you sure, Alison. Yea, yeah, okay, talk to you soon."

Drew jumped up. "What happened?"

"She was napping. Told me to call tomorrow. Can you wait until then?"

"Do I have a choice?" Drew's head hung low.

CHAPTER 11

Alison

What a summer. Alison had the chance to spend time with Tim. With her and Alan's busy schedule, they had to schedule time together. Now, that his season had started, she would have most days and night to herself. She made her way to the walk-in closet choosing a yellow maxi-dress and tan wedge heels. She would make up for the Sundays she hadn't been to church and meet Tonya.

The congregation was full of holy filled dancing, hands waving in mid-air. Some ran back and forth on the double-carpeted aisle. The pastor came with a message that was titled Greed. As they sat listening intently, Tonya however, kept talking about nothing. Did she know they were in church and not a club or some sort? Asia was quieter than she was. This began to irritate Alison. Just when she was politely to ask Tonya to hold her conversation until after service, the pastor called for invitation to discipleship. Tonya talked the entire time. Two women and a little boy came to be baptized. There was a great feeling when lost souls were found.

Moving along towards the exit, Alison looked at Tonya. "Hey, why don't you and Asia come over today? Alan will be back and we can all sit back and enjoy the rest of the day."

"Thank you." Happy, Tonya pulled Asia close. What time should we come?"

"Be there about 3 p.m. and don't forget to bring your bathing suits."

"Sure thing. We'll be there."

***

Alison tapped the entry button on her car remote system. Black iron gates with a large *P* on each slowly opened. She drove down the long twisting road admiring the colorful landscape. Her eyes widened when she saw Alan's car next to the garage. He was there. She slowly pulled into her space.

"Hey baby." He walked into the garage.

"Come here, I missed you." She hugged him tightly exhaling inaudible words.

"How was church?" He followed her into the kitchen.

"Church was good, but Tonya talked a lot during service."

"She did that when I went. I think she's just a talker."

"Maybe. You know I never asked her about her relationship status." Alison's fingers rested on her lips. "Did she tell you anything?"

Alan's head turned quickly. "No! Why would she tell me anything like that? Isn't that a girl's conversation?" He took a plate of salmon to the grill.

Alison followed quickly, "I'm just saying."

"No, Alison, she has not. I'm going to get the salmon started."

Alison stood in the gray and white contemporary kitchen. She took a cutlery board and sliced mangos, cilantro, tomatoes, and lime. Rice cooked. Refreshing Sangria would go well for the summer heat. A colorful display of fruit sat atop the glass patio table.

Patel colors dishware finished the table décor. Hands rested on her hips; Alison made her way to the bedroom. Removing her wedge heels, she lightly skipped from the coolness of the floor tile. She removed the dress and eyed her thin frame. Her laced panty and bra she let fall. With her hair pinned up, back to the mirror, she looked her bottom over. Suddenly, she remembered. Opening her make-up drawer shuffling a few things around, she found the small compact case. Her chest heaved up and down. She pushed the small pill through an aluminum opening allowing it to fall into her hands. Alison pulled a small flowered dixie cup from the dispenser, filled with water she swallowed the pill. As she wiped imaginary sweat from her forehead, Alan appeared.

"Baby you scared me." Alison dropped the case in the drawer.

Distracted by the nakedness of his wife Alan hadn't noticed, what had just happened. "What's taking you so long baby?"

"I was about to get in the shower." She exhaled. "Yes, let me get in."

"Not just yet." His arms wrapped her waist. "Mmm, baby you're so soft..."

She squirmed away. "Ah, baby, thank you, but we don't have time. Who is watching the grill?"

"Oh, damn." He pulled her close one last time. "I want this." He smacked her bottom.

"Tonight. If you're good." She stepped into the warm water.

Once Alan was out of sight, Alison peeked out, looked at the half-opened drawer, and sighed.

Tonya made it, 3 p.m. exactly, wearing a two-piece red, white, and blue bikini with a blue wrap. The suit accented Tonya's toned body. Asia had on a one-piece red suit and a pull over cover. Since they were dressed for swimming already Alison excused herself to change.

Alan took Tonya and Asia into the family room to go a few rounds on the video game. It had been a while since Alison wore the white two-piece swim suit Alan brought her. She would get all Alan's attention. She laughed thinking Miss Asia was going to have to fight for him. Asia took to Alan quickly and when they came to the house she jumped into his arms. Probably due to Asia not having her father around.

Alison stopped suddenly when she walked into the family room. Asia and Alan were into the video game and Tonya lay across the sofa as if she lived there. "Ahem." Alison cleared her throat. "I guess you're tired, Tonya."

"Oh, I'm sorry, girl, I was just relaxing. I didn't mean anything by it."

"Well, if you all are ready, we can either take that much needed dip in the pool or eat first. Asia, I'll let you decide."

She looked up at Alan with a smile. "I want to get into the pool."

"That's the final answer, let's go." Alison reached for Asia's and Alan's hand, leaving Tonya to walk alone.

Alan jumped in making a big splash. Once he swam a few seconds he reached for Asia and sat her on a floating duck.

Alison and Tonya sat in the lounge chairs sipping on the sangrias. They talked mostly about houses and designer clothing stores.

"You know, Alison, I envy you. You have a perfect marriage, the house and cars, but mostly a man to share it with."

"Girl…" She sipped on her drink. "You have no reason to be envious of me. You can have the same thing. You have that beautiful little girl who has captured Alan's heart."

Tonya smiled. "Yeah he does look happy. Are you guys trying to have a baby?"

"We have talked about it. It'll happened when it happens."

"Anyway, I want a good marriage and what comes with it, but Asia's father didn't have the same desire. He decided to join the military. Once he did, he forgot all about Asia and I. We didn't have the chance to even plan a wedding, let alone get engaged."

"Why would he do something like that? So, he has been gone for a while?"

"Yeah, he left after Asia was only three months old."

"I'm sorry. I didn't know."

Alison watched Alan and Asia then wiped tears from her eyes. Alison didn't know what she'd do if Alan had left her with a newborn baby. Probably hunt him down and kill him.

"Don't be sorry for me, Alison, I learned my lesson dealing with immature guys. That's what I wanted to talk to you about. I'm deciding on dating again and I do have someone in mind." She glanced over her shoulder.

"Oh, who is it? Someone from church or work?" She sat up.

"This guy, well, I want to keep it sort of quiet for now until I know he and I have something for sure." Her fingers gripped the glass tightly.

"What exactly happened between you and Asia's father?"

"Eric? That poor excuse of a father and lover for that matter. When we met, he was romantic and encouraging to me. After I found out I was pregnant, he changed. He started accusing me of trying to trap him into a relationship. I was deeply hurt by this. At first he was telling me how much he loved me and wanted a family."

"Did he have someone else on the side?"

"As he told me he didn't. I didn't suspect he did. Guess that's why it hurt me the way it did. Maybe if he said he did have another woman I could understand, but to up and leave after his beautiful baby girl was born puzzled me."

Alison patted Tonya's back. "Sometime men and women do things that we just can't explain. Have you been in contact with him much?"

"Alison." Tonya whispered.

Alison leaned in.

"Eric hit me—"

Alison whispered. "He hit you, Tonya, no way."

Tonya sipped her drink and continued, "Yes, he hit me. I was two months pregnant. He was accusing me this time of sleeping with his brother."

"Wow, did you guys fight often?" I mean it should never happen, but did you ever call the police?"

"I did, but I didn't press charges. I loved him. He is the father of my baby; I couldn't put him in jail."

"As long as you're away from that nut I suppose. It's in the past now."

They talked for another hour about the mystery guy and what Tonya should do to get him. Her eyes gleamed every time at the thought of this guy. Alison was getting just as excited because she knew how new love could be.

"What's his name? At least tell me that?"

Tonya put her hand on her chest looked at Alan before saying, "Daryl."

Alison repeated, "Daryl."

Alison grabbed Tonya's hand and walked toward the table. Alan and Alison ate small portions of the grilled fish, topped with the mango salsa, a spoonful of jasmine rice. Tonya took a bigger piece of the fish and toppings. Asia was more concerned with the assortment of fruit.

After dinner they all sat in the family room and watched cartoons with Asia. The adults jabbered about anything and everything. Three hours later, Alan excused himself to go for a run. He kissed Alison on the lips and rubbed her back, giving her a tingle. He made his way to Asia and gave her a hug.

In her baby voice she said, "Kiss."

He gave her a light peck on the cheek. It was Tonya's remark that darted Alison's eyes.

"Wow! Kisses going around. I didn't get mines."

Alan fidgeted with his shorts.

Tonya smiled. "You guys, I'm only joking. I'm sorry." She laughed, but it wasn't funny.

Alan disappeared into the corridor leaving the women alone.

"Alison, I'm sorry if I made you feel uncomfortable. My mother always told me that my mouth would get me into trouble, especially with women. I didn't mean anything by it, really." She seemed sincere. Alison let it pass…this time.

"Apology accepted, but don't go getting ideas from now on. Alan only kisses one woman." She half-laughed.

Eight p.m. had crept upon them. Asia drifted to sleep and Tonya decided to leave. Alison was exhausted, but more importantly she wanted her husband like never before. The women said their goodbyes and Alison went to the master bedroom. Alan lay across the bed, a sheet covering part of his nude body as he slept. He looked so peaceful; she couldn't disturb him. She showered and crawled slowly and quietly into the bed, cuddling next to her man. She listened to him breathe and smelled his showered fresh body.

CHAPTER 12

Alison

"Hey, baby girl, it's Tim."

"How are you?"

"Good. Listen I'm calling because I was literally forced to do this. I want you to hear me out and give it a try okay?"

"That depends. What is it, Tim?"

"We have a mutual friend and he's here waiting to talk to you."

A friend? Alison didn't know anyone who Tim knew to call a mutual friend.

"Well, who is it?"

"I'd rather put him on the phone. He has a lot to say to you. Give him a chance."

She let the word linger out, "Okay."

"Hello."

The voice was familiar, yet distance. She waited for more words to follow, but none did.

Alison asked, "Who is this?"

"Drew."

She gasped. Did her ears hear right? Such a long time since they spoke. She was so angry with him during their last conversation Alison had said unforgiving and demeaning words to Drew. When she walked away from him that day, his look of despair was compared to a man losing his loyal companion...the dog. She had wondered what happened to him.

"Alison?"

"I'm surprised to hear from you, Drew, and the fact you know Tim, but why the call?"

"I need to talk to you...set things straight and apologize again."

She wanted to hear what he had to say. She owed him that much. She loved Drew a long time ago, but hearing his voice brought back familiar feelings. The dead air on the phone gave her a warning that he was waiting as much as she to walk on uncharted grounds.

"Alison are you there?"

"Yes, I'm here."

Again, dead air. Then he answered, "Alison, I'm sorry for what happened years ago..."

"We already talked about this, Drew."

"No, you talked and I couldn't understand why you were so angry, but I found out later what really happened."

"What really happened?"

He explained and Alison couldn't believe what the back-stabbing Janice did. She made a mockery out of them. Of course, Drew was wrong, but Janice knew how much he cared for Alison so she had to make sure they wouldn't get back together. At the time, Alison, may have given Drew a chance to explain himself and just maybe, gotten back together.

"Drew, I'm sorry as well, but we were younger and a lot of pressure was out there. Something you didn't know, but I have always wondered about you. I care about you, but I also had to respect the fact that Alan was and still is here for me."

"Of course, you might not like this next shocker, but I married Janice."

She pulled the phone back and looked at it. "You *what*?"

"I know this is a shock, especially after what she did, but it wasn't until a few years later. I saw her and quite honestly, Alison, I think I married her because she was a part of this."

"Drew." Alison huffed. "Do you love her?"

"I do now, but I made a mess of things." He sighed.

The doorbell chimed. Alison looked at the monitor and saw Tonya's car at the gate. Buzzing Tonya through, she returned to the sofa.

All Alison heard was Drew rambling about sleeping with some girl at his job and possibly getting her pregnant.

"I tell you, Alison, I used a condom and I can't believe this is happening. She agrees that a baby wasn't for us at this moment, but then she went to my home and told Janice everything."

"Everything, ooh. Drew, I'm sorry, man, but you shouldn't have been messing around on your wife. I don't know what I'd do if I found out Alan did something so selfish."

"Well, you might want to show some concern because I need you right now."

What the…What was she supposed to do for him? Alan probably would kill her if he knew she was even talking to him.

"Janice put me out, that's why I'm here at Tim's. I can't stay here for long. I'm going to rent a studio apartment. All I want from you, Alison, is your ear. I really screwed up and since I found out Tim know you; it kicked some pain out of my life, but briefly. I told Tim there was someone I loved a long time ago and no one has taken her place. That's you." His voice trembled.

Alison, noticed Tonya with dark round rimmed sunglasses on, sitting in the garden. She caught a glimpse of Tonya wiping her face.

"Drew, I have to go, but listen call me later this evening or tomorrow. We could finish talking."

"Sounds good to me and Alison, thanks, for listening this much."

She pushed the red x and shoved her phone into her back pocket.

***

Alison removed her sandals letting her toes sink, becoming one with the grass. She sat next to Tonya on the sienna-colored stone bench overlooking a koi pond. Alison eyed Tonya's disheveled hair and bloodshot eyes.

"Alison." Tonya wailed out between sniffles. "Eric is taking me to court for Asia. He's trying to use the fact I'm single and financially unable to take care of her. The only reason it's so hard, he's not giving me one damn cent." She snatched a kleenex from her purse.

"Tonya, I strongly believe the judge won't order him custody because of that. What type of man takes a baby…little girl from her mother?"

"He's crazy like that. He makes me so angry when he does call. His wife took the phone, claiming he's a good father to her child and they could give Asia much more than I can." She pointed to the pond. "Some nerve that high-strung black bitch telling me that. The tramp hasn't been around long enough to know him." Her head dropped.

"Where is he living?"

"Would you believe he's here? They had a home built near Stone Mountain. He's still serving time in the military as a reservist and working full-time at a government agency. She's doing pretty well, an insurance broker."

"I know this hurt—"

"You damn right it does. And men wonder why women can be crazy bitches when dealing with their trifling asses."

Wide eyed, Alison looked around the pond hoping a response would jump right out.

"Maybe Eric isn't happy in his current marriage and wants company in his misery."

"That bastard should suffer whatever comes his way."

"You don't mean that."

"Oh, but I do. And I don't want her to be any type of mother to my child."

"She only told you what she thinks her husband is capable of. I don't think she meant to be disrespecting. You two need to get along, especially if the judge order joint custody."

"Alison." Tonya's puffed and red eyes hovered, "What if Alan left you for another woman?"

How could Tonya ask her that? She never gave thought to something so foolish, but what would she do?

"Alison." Tonya's gaze darted into Alison's eyes.

"I don't know, Tonya." She sighed heavily. But I'll pray."

"So, you think praying will help? God don't answer prayers." Tonya laughed hysterically.

Alison knew Tonya was having a hard time right now, but she was letting her faith be affected. That was if she ever had any.

"Yes, I know praying will help. God does answer prayers, maybe not when we want, but he's always on time. We have to endure trials so we don't forget that he is there for us. If we had good all the time, would we ever pray and say thank you?"

Tonya waved her hands in the air, "Whatever. I don't want to hear this right now."

"If that's what you want—"

"It is!" Tonya stared deeply and long at Alison.

"Okay, then on a better note, how's things with Daryl, the guy you told me about?"

Like the character Samantha from Bewitched, Tonya twisted the corner of her lip upward. "He's Alan's friend from the team."

Alison batted her eyes with mouth opened. Daryl was not the committed type of guy. Hopefully Tonya knew what she was getting into.

"So, what do you think of him, Alison?"

Alison watched how Tonya's tears disappeared and her eyes now had life in them. "I call him a big bear. I'm surprised. Alan never mentioned this to me, neither has Daryl.'

Tonya lowered her eyes, "I asked Daryl not to say anything yet. I wanted us to get better acquainted. You understand that, right."

"Have you guys done anything exciting?" Alison smiled and gyrated her hips.

"Really? No, but I'm planning on it." Tonya gyrated back and lifted her arms. "Do you trust Alan?"

"Trust Alan? Of course, I do. Why wouldn't I?"

"Come on, Alison, all those fans and his traveling. I would be worried if that was my husband."

"I trust him, but not the hoochies." Alison laughed. Her side ached. "I've been through those stages of insecurity back in high school and college."

Tonya sucked her bottom lip. "You should be a little more open to the idea Alan is a *man_*and weak by nature. He can only put up a shield for so long before he arms get weak and brings it down."

Alison's fingers found a few strands of hair and twirled. "Why are you saying this? I wouldn't say anything like that to you if you had a decent man in your life." Alison said with a slight roll of her head.

"Come on, Alison, don't get an attitude. I'm talking as a friend. I wouldn't want to see you get hurt because you choose to be naïve on the matter. What if Alan did have an affair? That would devastate you, right?"

"Yes."

"If you kept an open mind about all this, it wouldn't hurt as much?"

"Thanks for the advice, Tonya, but I don't need it. I know my husband and he love me enough not to stray to some lonely, disrespecting, home-wrecking woman. Don't you forget that." Alison fumed as she held back wicked thoughts of Alan cheating on her.

"Alison, I'm sorry." She placed her hands on Alison's shoulders and tears filled her eyes. I don't know why I have been so careless with my words lately. I guess I'm letting this Eric thing get to me. You're a good person and I'm sorry."

"Do you want to come in have some lemonade?" Alison offered as they walked towards the house.

"No, thank you. I'm going home. I need some me time right now."

As she turned, her high-heeled sandals clicked and clanked against the canyon stone acid stained driveway.

The evening had come quick as a one-hit wonder show Alison was watching on cable. Alone and sad, she sat in the family room. She started to cry, but couldn't figure out why. She grabbed a picture of Alan and her standing near the Disney World entrance, pulled her knees to her chest and rocked slowly back and forth. She got up, paced the room, then sat back down. All she kept thinking was what Tonya said. "He's a man and weak." It hurt her to even think that. Was she being naïve? He could be with someone as she sat there alone.

The game, over hours ago, she hadn't heard from Alan. Every time she called, his voicemail spoke to her. The ritual was, Alison would always get a call if only for a few minutes. Today was different. Her bones ached as she paced the floor again. Then she remembered, Alan, was stand-offish when she returned from New York.

"My God, don't do this to me. Don't put my marriage through this kind of test!" Alison screamed.

The phone rang. "Hey, baby, I miss you."

Hearing Alan's voice made the tears come back. "I miss you too, Alan and I love you."

"Baby are you okay?"

"No." She sniffed. "I mean, yes. I'm okay. I want you to come home."

"Baby, don't scare me like that. I'll be home tonight."

"I love you Alan."

"I love you too. Baby, I have to go. Love and kisses."

Alison smiled as she looked at the picture that was cradled against her chest. She went to the bathroom. Showered, with her fingers, fluffed her hair, spritzed floral fragrance and brushed her teeth. Giving herself a once over look in the mirror, her naked body strolled to the bed. Too early for sleep, she picked up a best seller, *Indiscretions*, flipped to her bookmark and read.

About an hour into reading, she heard a distant ringing. Her cell phone tucked deeply in the trendy purse. Alison tossed the covers back and sprinted across the room.

"Hello." Alison touched the screen.

"Hey. It's me, Drew. Did I wake you?"

"No, I was reading. It's a good novel. I was about to get to the steamy sex scenes."

"Ah, you're still reading books."

"Every chance I get. Is Tim asleep?"

"Yes, he needs his rest you know with—"

"With what, Drew?"

"Nothing. How has your day been?"

"You wouldn't believe what I was asked today and told." She said as of matter fact. "But I don't think I should talk to you about this."

"Alison, I don't want anything from you. I don't want to mess up your marriage either. I thought we were going to put the past behind us and become friends again?"

"We are but…" She didn't know how to confide in Drew of her insecurities. After all she bragged about Alan to his face.

"But what?" Drew's voice low and tranquil.

"Okay, here goes." She exhaled forcefully. "Tonya, I met her a couple months ago and she asked me what would I do if Alan cheated on me?"

"What did you say?"

"I told her I'll pray about it. She also claims all men are weak and will slip eventually. I think she was venting because her baby daddy wants custody of their daughter. What do you think?"

Alison didn't know what was up with her phone lines, but everyone seemed to get pretty damn quiet when serious questions were asked. "Did I not speak loud enough, Drew?"

"Look, Alison, do you really want to hear what I have to say?"

"I do."

"I'm going to be straight with you. Alan and I never got along true, but I wouldn't say anything bad about him if I didn't think it was true. I'm a man and look where it's got me, put out of my house. Some of us men, try very hard to be faithful, but we fail. We don't mean to, but it happens. My case is different. I think I wanted to screw around on Janice because I was angry for her participation in breaking us up. I somehow wanted her to feel the hurt I felt all these years. Alan? I know he loves you, but it's always a possibility. If given the right moment, I'm positive he would."

"Really, Drew?"

"You asked me. Look, he loves you and he'll be a damn fool to mess that up."

He was right. Some men make the mistake of bed hopping, but she sincerely hoped that her husband had more sense than a dog in heat, humping whatever came along just because.

"Drew, I'm sorry for what happened years ago too. I have wondered if we were together how things would be." Alison sighed. "But that was a long time ago."

"So, you missed me too?"

Alison breathed heavy. "Are you hard of hearing?" She chuckled. "I have, but I also moved on, with Alan. You'll always be in my heart. But Alan is my heart."

"I hear you and I'm definitely not trying to open a pandora's box. All I wanted to do was have your forgiveness and figure out what I'm going to do with my life."

"Drew, you'll be fine. If you are sincerely sorry for what you did to Janice it'll work out. I know you're a good person and you'll have all your life to make it up to her."

Lying across the giant-sized bed, Alison wide-eyed, stared out the skylight into the star-filled midnight sky, erasing any and all thought of negativity.

CHAPTER 13

Alan

As they rode in the limousine listening to Usher's song, Alan flinched each time he heard the word confessions belt from the speakers. That horrible night in the hotel with Daryl and those women was embedded in his mind. He and Daryl never followed up as to why they were drugged and left with their clothes down.

"Daryl, you gave any thought about that night?"

"What night?"

Alan starred at his teammate. "At the hotel." His eyes darted left to right.

"Nope, ain't trying to, and neither should you." Daryl rocked his head now to a Taylor Swift song.

"Come on, man, you act like it's nothing to worry about. Those damn women did something to us and I'm quite sure we'll pay for it later."

"Alan, you are one paranoid dude. Is that how ya'll Mississippi boys are?" Daryl fist bumped his shoulder.

"It doesn't sit well with me, that's all. Damn, if Alison finds out what happened she'll probably kill my ass."

This time a growl of a laugh escaped Daryl. "You scared of yo woman too. Oh, oh, I get it, she got you whooped, huh?"

"Fuck you, Daryl. This is all about respect. I love my wife, man, I really do."

"I'm sorry, Alan, I guess I let my selfishness get in the way. You right about respect, that's your wife and I do understand, believe me. Because I'm single it's hard for me at times to take things seriously. I'm not trying to get involved with anyone and be tied down." Alan gave a quick glanced and Daryl continued, "I don't mean anything bad about your situation it's just not for me."

"I know, man…you cool, thanks for the honesty."

The limousine pulled up to the black iron gates, Alan reached out and with a few taps the gates opened. The limousine slowly hugged the winding road as to caress each curve. At the front entrance the vehicle stopped.

"Hey, give me a call later tomorrow, I want some time with Alison."

"I hear you, holla."

They slammed their fist into one another and Alan was gone.

He knew by the darkness and quietness Alison was upstairs maybe asleep. He tiptoed up the floating staircase carrying a bouquet of red, white, and yellow roses and champagne. Quietly, he walked down the corridor toward the master bedroom. Light from the tv escaped through a slightly ajar door. Alan peeked in at his wife sleeping peacefully. Laying the roses on the nightstand, he gently sat beside Alison, caressing her naked body. He lowered his head to her perfumed neck and kissed gently, still holding the champagne. As he touched her soft body his manhood screamed for her love.

In a light whisper Alison spoke. "Alan, is that you?"

"Yeah, baby, it's me. I wanted to surprise you, but you looked so peaceful." He kissed her forehead. "Look what I have for you?" He grabbed the roses and held the champagne bottle up.

Alison sat up, hugged and kissed her husband passionately. "Alan, they are beautiful." She reached for the roses and inhaled. "I'm glad you're here, I can sleep better now."

"Yes, Baby, I'm here and you can sleep all night long in my arms." He sat the bottle on the nightstand. I'm going to take a quick shower then…"

"Then what?" she inched closer opening her legs.

"Get the glasses and we toast to…love. Then we'll see what happens." Clothes fell as he neared the bathroom.

Alan stepped from the bathroom with misty steam behind him. His eyes locked on Alison. A few droplets glistened on his muscular body. His walk tall and steady, reached Alison. He climbed gently on top of her. Alan buried his head between her breasts. He sat up, rubbed her arms, slowly caressed her stomach, and squeezed her thighs.

He licked her perfumed thighs. Extending her long legs, he continued licking down to her feet. He sucked each of her neatly polished toes. He worked his way back to Alison's hot spot and blew light breaths. Alison arched her back slightly, giving him more access.

He spread her legs wider and let his head become relaxed into the moist of his wife. Alan held onto her body as he continued feverishly. Though Alison was a tall woman, compared to his six two height, she felt tiny to him.

"Alison, you want me to stop?"

"No, baby, keep going...it's good."

"Damn good, right?" He gently bit her.

"Yes, Alan, yes!"

"I feel you Alison, you right there, let it go, baby, let it go. I want to feel your warmth all over my face." Alan held her tighter with each intense moment.

"Alan...uh...please..." Alison grabbed her husband's head, holding it steady.

"Let it go, girl." He pushed in deeper with his tongue while his finger played tricks.

"Aah, Alan...aah it feels good..." She exhaled and her legs tightened around his head. Once her body stopped dancing, Alan released her.

"You okay, baby." He snuggled against her.

"Boy, I could slap the taste from your mouth that felt so damn good, ooh I don't know what to do." She squeezed his arms and cradled more into him.

"I'm glad you like it…I aim to please."

"Don't you want me to return the favor or something?"

"Not at all. This was for you, I'm cool."

"I knew there was a reason I loved you so much."

CHAPTER 14

Alison

The sun shined and the weather forecast was predicted to be a hot and humid day. Alison cradled the cell phone between her shoulder and neck.

"Tonya, I wish I could talk longer, but I'm leaving for a trip?"

"A trip? Another one? Didn't Alan just get home?"

'Wow.' Alison thought. Could Tonya have asked any more questions. She wanted to be home with her husband too. But their schedules had now overlapped.

"He came home a few nights ago. Work calls, I have to make my money." She flipped through a make-up case.

"I was thinking we could get together for a girl's day. Lunch."

With a light peach blush, Alison applied it to her cheeks and a swiped down her nose. She fluffed her eyelashes with a waterproof black mascara. Reaching further into her make-up bag, she lined her lips and smoothed on a peach and amber lipstick. She moved her lips in and out then gave a smack.

"Lunch will be good. So, did you get to spend some time with Daryl?"

"Girl, no. He doesn't seem interested."

"Really?"

"Mmph, nope, not at all."

"That's weird. He seems like a guy that wants to date."

"That's okay. I have gone this long without a man; I can continue on. But, the va jay jay does need some attention."

The ladies laughed.

"I know what you mean. Listen Tonya I have to go, we'll talk when I get back."

Alison stuffed the remaining make-up essentials in her shoulder bad. Walking to the nightstand she slipped into a pair of blue skinny jeans, white halter top, and a pair of white tennis shoes. Her hair was twisted and pinned up with a few strands straddling her long neck. Her large hooped silver earrings dangled while she looks herself over. Satisfied with her look, she grabbed the large shoulder bag.

"Alison are you ready?"

She heard Alan approaching. "Yes, dear."

"Hey." He kissed her. "I'm going to miss you."

"I'll miss you more."

They walked hand-in-hand down the corridor.

Alison's feet anchored to the floor. "Baby, I forgot something, go on down, I'll meet you."

Alan brows furrowed, "Okay."

She smiled, walked back to the bedroom, while watching Alan. Alison sighed a sense of relief. She fumbled in the bathroom drawer, found her case, pushed a pill through the foil, and popped it in her mouth. As she turned the dixie cup of water up, her eyes met Alan's. Still holding the case in her hand, she sat the cup down slowly.

"What the fuck is that?" He pointed to her hand.

Should she lie? Should she act ignorant to what he was asking? Her stomach entertained butterflies.

She looked at the case and with her eyes down, "My birth control pills."

There were no words between them. She could feel the hurt and deceit she has caused.

"Birth control pills? What? Wait…"

"Alan, I'm sorry." She sighed. "I'm not ready for a family and honestly I don't think I want to have children."

"So, you sneak behind my back taking this shit." He snatched the case from her and hurled it across the room.

Alison startled, "Sneak? I wasn't sneaking, I—"

"What the hell do you call it? We talked about this and—"

"Actually, you talked about it. True, I wasn't upfront and honest with you. I lead you to believe that someday we would start a family, but after our anniversary dinner, I, I just don't think I want to."

She could smell the anger; Alan was close to her. Looking up into his eyes, she saw hues of red settled with water. Alan stepped back from her and turned his back.

"Why don't you call a car to take you to…" He wiped his face.

She reached for him. He moved further away.

"Alan, baby, I'm so sorry. We are happy with the two of us. We can do so much in life; do we really need a baby?"

Alison saw the nostrils flare out and in. She never seen her husband this angry or hurt.

"You need to go Alison. I can't be around you right now."

She pulled out her phone and called a car. She felt weak dragging the shoulder bag behind her. When she reached the corridor, she looked back to her husband. She just struck him down, by his Achilles heel, a baby.

***

Alison leaned into the plush leather seats. No appetite for her. Couldn't sleep. Her hair stylist Chantay sat comfortably besides her reading a style magazine. Alison tucked her personal travel pillow behind her head and closed her eyes. She took in the silence that surrounded her, then the common noise…the plane engines, small chatter from nearby passengers, food carts pushed by flight attendants, and Chantay flipping through her magazine.

The soothing sound of the engine began to hypnotized Alison. Sleep over came her. Her dream was of a pond surrounded by beautiful red, yellow, and white roses. The money green grass was tall and shifting with the wind. She stood next to Alan. He looked at her and rubbed her stomach. She rubbed his back and lay her head on his shoulder. In the pond she saw two over-sized gold fish swimming freely. Just as she turned to kiss Alan the sky turned grayish black, with clouds twirled within the mixture. Lightning struck inches from them. Alan pulled away from her, running to a figure in the distance. Alison cried out to him. No response. Rain poured down, drenching her. Roses once beautiful turned black, the goldfish died, and Alan stopped running. Alison called out again to him. He turned to her, smiled, and waved. Her stomach in unbearable pain, Alison fell to her knees. One hand on her stomach the other planted against the wet ground. She cringed and frowned in excruciating pain…Alan's departure with someone other than her and the pain she now endured.

Slowly she managed to stand and grass stained with blood…her blood, covered the white dress. Something hung between her legs, she couldn't figure out what. She looked up and, in the distance, again she saw Alan and the figure holding what appeared to be a baby. They pointed and laughed at her before disappearing again…this time for good.

"No, God, please."

"Wake up." Chantay shook Alison.

Alison shook and wiped her eyes. She looked at Chantay. "I'm sorry." She shook her head. "I had a strange dream." She turned toward the window.

"You okay, girl?"

"I'm fine."

"You want to talk about it?"

"No, I don't want to talk about it. Will you just mind your own damn business?"

"Okay." Chantay let the words linger. "You know what, you better apologized because that wasn't called for."

Alison knew it wasn't called for. Childish. The way Chantay demanded an apology didn't warrant Alison to move quickly, instead she pushed the attendant button and turned back to the window.

"Yes, ma'am, can I help you?"

"A bottle of water please and thank you."

"Aren't you something," Chantay tearfully began. "I was only trying to help you and you act like this with me. What in the hell did I do to you? I've been working with you over two years now and never have you spoke to me like this."

"Chantay, I'm sorry. The dream I had…very strange—"

"I don't need to know, but thank you for the apology." Chantay continued flipping through the magazine.

At the Grand Hotel & Suites in Toronto, the bell boy strutted behind wheeling both her and Chantay's designer luggage. They would share the two-bedroom suite with two full marble bathrooms a full kitchen, living room, and patio. Alison actually enjoyed having her in the same room. Chantay wouldn't have to lug around her tools. They would sit up all night after a long day of shooting and talk about any and everything. Strange thing though outside of work Alison and Chantay never hung out. Chantay would occasionally style Alison long mane for special occasions, but that was the extent of their friendship.

Alison ventured into the kitchen and prepared a small pot of French vanilla coffee.

"Chantay when you're done unpacking can I speak with you?"

"No problem, boss." Chantay chuckled.

She held the small cup of steaming coffee and inhaled the aroma. She sipped, sat down Indian style on the sofa, and stared at the phone.

She sat the cup on the table reached for her phone. She went to her favorites list and pressed Alan's name. Alison listened as the continuous rings belted through. She hit the red x button and repeated the cycle. Three times she had tried to call Alan. Her phone chirped. She looks down and a message appeared in a green bubble.

"I'm busy. Going out tonight with Daryl." The message read.

Alison huffed…

"So, what did you want to talk about?"

"Chantay, I know I already apologized on the plane, but I'm really sorry how I spoke to you. That wasn't called for and I'm sorry."

"Don't worry about it. Is something bothering you?"

"No-no everything is fine." Waving her hand, Alison tried to laugh it off, but she knew Chantay didn't believe it. Chantay never dug into Alison's personal life. If she didn't offer information, Chantay didn't ask.

CHAPTER 15

Drew

Drew was happy that Alison had listened to him. He was glad she was happy even though he wasn't a part of her life the way he wanted. Just to know that she knew the truth of their break-up made him feel like he could now move on. The first thing he had to do was figure out what to do about Mallory. He didn't love her or the child she was carrying. He knew his uncaring attitude about his love child was sad and disgraceful.

Days at work for Drew were long and suffering. He couldn't avoid Mallory. He caught the wicked stares of her drama-filled, male-bashing, trampy friends. Office gossip was surely not on Drew's agenda, but somehow, he had to make it go away.

"Mallory, could you come into my office please." Drew fidgeted with a pen, making circles on his desk calendar. What did he have to lose now since his wife put him out? He studied the grooves in the ceiling, never noticing they were there. He stood with his hands in a praise position and closed his eyes.

"Hey, Drew." Each word slowly slithered from Mallory's lips. "You wanted to see me?"

"Damn, Mallory, you could've knocked."

"I did, guess you were thinking about something."

"We need to talk. First, I want to apologize how I spoke to you the last time you were in here. I was wrong and selfish."

"Drew, honey, you don't have to apologize and I understand it was a shock to hear you are going to be a father. Drew cringed. She rubbed her flat stomach and continued, "By someone other than your wife. I'm the one who should be sorry for going to her with the news, but—"

"Look, the damage is done, Janice put me out."

Her eyes widened. "Are you serious?"

"Don't act surprised, it's probably what you wanted, but that doesn't mean I want to be away from her. I love her, Mallory…that's my wife."

"What about me, our baby, or us?"

The tension grew more and both stood in a combative stance. With the back of his hand Drew wiped his mouth, while Mallory clasped her hands together.

"I don't know how to say this, but to say it…I'm not leaving my wife."

"Oh yeah, so you just fuck me, get me pregnant, and vanish from my life. You ain't nothing, but a no good—"

"I'll choke the living shit out of you, stupid bitch. Don't you ever fix your mouth to call me anything other than my name." His eyes bulged and arms stretched before him.

Mallory scurried across the room. Her cheeks turned rose red and her blue eyes were lost in a sea of tears. "Drew, please, I'm sorry don't hurt me."

"Please, you ain't worth hurting. All I wanted to say, I will be a part of our baby life, but you and I, we can't have a relationship other than co-parent this baby."

She buried her face in her hands. He didn't know if it was angry crying or happy. She was a total nut case at times. She wiped her eyes, looked at Drew, smiled, and turned to leave. He exhaled, sat down, and began working.

Mallory held her head up. "Drew, I can live with that…you being a part of our baby's life. I promise to stay off your back and work with you on raising the baby and working together." She wiped her eyes, sniffled, and laughed. "I'm sorry for my behavior."

How was Drew to accept her monumental apologies? She scared him, but he would never let her know it. He knew one thing—he should've listened to Tim and stayed the hell away from her, now he had a case of two women scorned.

"All right, Mallory, we'll talk later I have a lot of work to do and I know you do as well." He smiled.

Mallory walked toward the door and stopped, without turning around she whispered, "I'm really sorry."

***

"Come on man, let's, go shoot hoops." Tim rushed in Drew's office.

"Slow your speed, dog. I'm really not into it today. I talked with Mallory—"

"You trying to get in her bed again?"

"Get serious, Tim, I've learned my lesson. Man, she's crazy. She cries one minute then cursing my ass out the next." Drew chuckled. "She apologize too much. Makes me wonder if she's up to something again. I really don't know how to take her. I don't want to hurt her like this, but what she did was bullshit and you know it."

"Don't put all the blame on her, Drew. If you weren't screwing everything that walked you wouldn't be in this mess."

"You taking up for her? Regardless of what I did, she didn't have to go to my wife. She knew the condition of our relationship."

"So, you had a relationship?"

What's your fucking problem, Tim, huh, what? Maybe you're jealous because you didn't get some of that coochie. For the last time, she knew I wasn't interested in having a committed relationship, how could I, being married. She just wanted a piece of me just like I wanted of her…that's all."

They stood tall and broad at each other, nostrils opened and fists clenched. Life dealt them both a handful of hearts, which were made to be broken.

"Tim, Tim, what are we doing? We arguing like bitches, come on, dog, you my boy, we don't need this. I understand everything you're saying, but you have to know we're different on some things and I have my opinion."

Tim reached for Drew's hand, "You're right, let's squash this nonsense and go shoot some hoops. Good thing you drove today, I really didn't feel like making a trip in the cab."

Through stand-still traffic to reach West End Sports Club, it took the guys thirty minutes. Drew flashed his membership Id to the security guard and proceeded into the underground parking.

"I'm glad we're here, Tim. I need to release some stress and not the old-fashioned way, if you know what I mean. "Drew slipped on his blue and white shorts.

"Good. I'm ready to whoop your butt on the court."

"Bring it on, man, bring it on."

CHAPTER 16

Alan

"Hey man you need to hook-up with Tonya, Alison's girl." Alan squinted at Daryl.

"I ain't trying to get involved with some money-hungry groupie, man." Daryl flicked his hand in the air.

"She's not like that, man. You should see her, she's ta-da-bam, fine as hell. Between us, if I wasn't married, I'll get with her." He swallowed frothy beer.

"Naw, dog, not you the faithful, choir boy, God almighty type. Alison must have pissed you off?" Daryl hit Alan on the back.

"She did. We had a small argument before she left and I haven't spoke to her since. She's called. I text her I was going out tonight."

"What you do, Alan?"

"I didn't do anything except tell her I wanted us to start a family."

"That's it?"

"She lied to me. Or rather lead me on all these years. You know excuse after excuse. First, she wanted to wait to get her career going. Okay, I get that—"

"Let me guess, she doesn't want any kids now?"

Alan turned, hit Daryl in the chest. "Exactly. She says we can be happy just us two."

"I wish you luck on that Alan. Maybe she'll come around."

"I doubt it. She was taking the pill. I thought she had stopped and this morning, I caught her."

"Oh, snap! Wow." Daryl placed a closed fist up to his mouth.

Alan swallowed big gulps of his beer. Once the bottle was empty, he waved the bartender for another. Hours passed and the drinks began to consume Alan. He was going to live it up tonight since Daryl was the designated driver. As he tipped the last of five bottles up, he eyes widened. Before him stood a bronze, glowing goddess. He smiled. She smiled and walked towards him.

"What's up, man what are you looking at?" Daryl glanced over his shoulder.

"Ahem. My dear friend, the woman, I was talking about is on her way over here."

Daryl wiped his mouth and stood to greet her. "You must be Tonya. I'm Daryl."

"Hmm, I must be a hot topic if you know who I am." She glanced toward Alan.

"Oh yeah, he told me about you. As a matter of fact, he was just saying how he would like to—"

Alan nearly choked on his beer. "Hey Tonya, what are you doing here?" He quickly diverted Tonya's attention away from Daryl.

"I had to get out. Tired of sitting in the house, so I hired a babysitter and here I am." She twirled and ordered a drink.

Alan offered her his seat at the bar. He watched the arch of her back as her breast and butt stuck out as she sat. As she crossed her legs, Alan watched each seductive move. He swallowed hard. Her black skirt inched up more as she adjusted it. The strapless black and white striped top showed her beautiful, smooth cocoa shoulders. The large gold hoop earrings glistened against her skin and wide bangle bracelets adorned her wrists. He followed her legs, admiring the tone. Her thin-strapped sandals had to be at least five inches. The thought of her standing over him in them…

"Alan, did you hear me?" Tonya poke him in the shoulder.

He shook his head. "What? No. I was thinking."

"When will Alison be back." She licked a cherry from her Mai Tai drink.

Alan stuttered. "Next week or so. After she's done in Canada she's going to Spain."

"Wow, that's interesting. I think I've could've modeled; don't you guys think so?"

Both Alan and Daryl quickly said yes. The night oozed by with more drinking and the three of them getting closer.

"Daryl, why aren't you drinking?" Tonya leaned into him.

"I have to make sure my buddy here gets home okay and by the way it looks you need to put a hold on it too."

"I'm fine...I took an uber."

Alan drunk or not was always a gentleman. "Well, I'm quite sure we can give you a ride home...you don't need to be in a cab with some strange, horny dude."

"Maybe not strange, but horny I'll take." She licked her lips again focusing on Alan. "If you'll excuse me gentlemen, I have to use the lady's room."

Alan helped her down from the stool and watched her walk away.

Daryl yanked Alan's arm. "She's fine as hell, Oh, how I would love a chance at her, but she wants you."

"Naw, she's flirty. Tonya doesn't want me."

"Bullshit! Who you fooling...I see the way you two look at each other and I really don't care if you go for it or not, but I think you should. One time won't hurt. I got your back, if you want to, we men have to stick together. A fine specimen like that come to me and *I* was married I'll have to get with her just once."

Alan rubbed his head and asked the bartender for two tall glasses of water. He placed his hands on the bar and stood in silence. The music and chatter were overwhelmed by the words of Daryl, "One time."

"Alan, what man haven't strayed. It's in our genes. To be honest, if you hit it and can talk me into getting some from her hey…"

Alan moved close to Daryl. "I've told you; Tonya isn't like that and I wouldn't allow that to happen."

"You wouldn't allow that." Daryl mocked Alan. "You do care for her."

"Daryl, please. I don't think she should be played like that. For crying out loud she comes to my home, I play with her daughter, and I guess by her being around I naturally care."

"Like I said before, if I can't get any, you should go for it, you'll thank me later." Daryl patted Alan on the back.

"Thank you later…what about that fucking party we were ruffied at with a bunch of gay women. We don't even know what that was all about."

"Obliviously nothing. Like you say, a bunch of gay women probably wanted to see some real men packages, you know what I mean?" Daryl's mouth took a sideways slant. "A few more rounds and you want to be up?"

"Are we going to give her a ride home?"

"Where ever you like." Daryl's eyebrows arched up.

Tonya had returned with refreshed lipstick and brushed her hair. The music had slowed and people intertwined together on the dance floor.

"Excuse me, Daryl, may I borrow your friend for a dance."

"He's all yours."

Without hesitation Alan took Tonya by the arm then cupped her around the waist. Alan pulled her closely and allowed her head to lie comfortable on his chest. Her perfume enticed his nostrils. He breathed heavily and hugged her tighter. Alan stroked her hair. He lightly rubbed her face and brushed his finger across her lips.

After the song, Alan waved. "Daryl, I think we're ready to leave."

Daryl winked at him and the three headed to the car.

"So where to?" Daryl looked at Tonya then turned to the back seat where Alan sat.

"My house," Alan said quietly. "I want to talk to Tonya. I'll take her home later."

"Your wish is my command."

Alan watched as cars sped by. He barely heard Tonya's and Daryl's conversation.

***

Alan and Tonya walked through the kitchen into the family room. They sat on opposite ends of the sofa and stared.

Tonya smiled and asked, "Mind if I take my shoes off?"

Alan's arm stretched out on the sofa. "Go ahead get comfortable." Unconsciously he licked his lips.

Tonya moved closer to Alan. "What did you want to talk to me about?" She rubbed his arm.

"There's no doubt that we want to get with each other, but I'm married, Tonya, and you're friends with my wife."

"I understand, believe me." She squeezed his arm. I'm not trying to cause problems in your relationship. I enjoy talking with you and yes, I am attracted to you. I cannot help myself, when I look at you, your smile and physique get the best of me. Never have I done anything to give any interest in you to Alison. I like her."

"I know you do, but you have to understand I love her."

"Alan, one thing you can count on is my loyalty as a friend. I don't want to hurt neither one of you." She placed his hand in her lap. "Alan, do you want to kiss me?"

"In all honesty I want to do more."

CHAPTER 17

Drew

Drew felt it was time for him to put an end to Janice's unforgiving ways and move back in. He was gone long enough for her to get over the small mistake he made and work out whatever problems lay before them, one being Mallory, the other his love child. He felt like a stranger at his own home, having to ring the doorbell and wait to be escorted in. Janice had agreed that it was time they talk and try to resolve the matter.

"Hey, baby, you look good." Drew stood at the door, waiting to be escorted.

"Come in, Drew."

He smelled pot roast with carrots, potatoes, onions and mushrooms, simmered in thick brown gravy. They walked to the large kitchen and Drew saw the nice table. A bowl of buttered rolls and a pitcher of sweet tea.

"Wow, this looks good what's the occasion?" Drew laughed.

"Drew, at this point I'm not in a laughing mood. I cooked dinner because I feel sorry for your cheating black ass. I know you have not had a good meal since you have been gone, so least, I could do is this. I'm not a bad person, Drew, which brings me to the question of why you couldn't remain faithful to me."

He did not expect the conversation to start so soon, but was relieved that Janice cared enough to cook him a meal.

"Janice, this is going to be a long night because I have a lot to tell you and I really want to work this out. I miss you."

"You can start by telling me what you're going to do about that baby your girlfriend is carrying."

"She's not my girlfriend and I'm going to be part of the baby's life."

"What?" Janice batted her eyelids. "You tell me you want to work it out, but you going to remain in that bitch's life."

"This is not easy. I did not want to, I asked her to get an abortion, she agreed, but we know now…she lied. I told her I did not want any part of it, but honestly, what kind of man does that make me. I screwed up. The baby is innocent. It took me a while to convince myself of this."

Janice put a big helping of roast on Drew's plate and set the basket of hot buttered rolls in front of him. "How do you expect me to handle this, Drew? How can we go on and have that woman in our lives? I don't think she's going to roll over and die, since she had the nerves to show up here."

"We shouldn't expect her to roll over and die, yet you support me and the child. Rather, could you accept the baby?"

"I don't know. I really don't know at this point. I have thought about this since you've been gone, but I don't know if it's going to hurt us or be a blessing?"

"We'll make it a blessing. I told Mallory that I love you and I want to be with you. Of course, she blew up at first, but she said she understood, just as long as I have a part in our baby's life."

"This feels awkward to hear you say 'our baby' with someone else. This will take a long time for me to get used to."

He reached across the table for her hand, but reluctantly she pulled it back. He was asking a lot of Janice, but he wasn't finished with his repentance.

"This dinner is great. You really didn't have to go through the trouble."

"I never stopped loving you, Drew. It hurt me to put you out, but I had to."

"There's something else we need to talk about."

"You screwed someone else?"

"I talked to Alison." Drew looked Janice straight into the eyes for any signs of shock. Instead, she kept her head down, chewing.

"Did you hear me, Janice?"

"Yes. Why and how did you talk to her?"

"Long story short, she's friends with Tim. I asked him to call her."

Janice never looked up, but continued eating. "Why?"

"You know why. All these years Alison thought I broke off our relationship and I never felt right about that. I wanted her to know the truth."

"Other words you still love her and wanted her to know I was the jealous girlfriend." Janice eyes finally met Drew's.

"Truth…I loved her for a long time, I thought it was going to be she and I married, having the nice house, cars, and kids, but it didn't turn out that way because of what you did."

How are you going to blame some college shit on me? You and her probably wouldn't have made it far anyway because of Alan. What girl then, could resist him?"

"That's not the point. I had a chance."

"What exactly are you saying, Drew? You want me to apologize to Alison, you can forget it. You are asking me to accept that girl's baby and you back into my life. Alison is a big girl and doing well, she doesn't need my apology."

"Actually, I apologized for you and Alison was forgiving as I expected she would be."

"So why did you even bring this up? You could've left that out."

"I blamed what you did…for my behavior. I wanted you to hurt in some way because all these years I hurt. It's not an excuse for what I have done, but it's what I felt. That's why I'm here—to apologize for everything I have done. Alison forgave me…that was one part of my life I needed to set free. Now I'm asking you to forgive me. I want to change, Janice, I really do. I want to be the husband you always wanted. I want to make things right between us."

Drew sat back in the soft, chair and watched Janice slowly bite into a dinner roll. Her poise touched his soul. She was a good woman, but years past she let jealousy get the best of her, which stirred an event of wrongful doings. He couldn't blame this entirely on Janice. If only he had been mature and thoughtful of his actions.

"Janice, I'm sorry, baby, I never should have slept with that girl. I do love you and you have to believe that. Alison is my past…she's happy and that's where I'm trying to get with you—happiness."

Janice put her fork down, sipped the ice-tea, and let her eyes linger on Drew. "How can I trust you, Drew? You defiled our marriage by taking the most intimate thing between us and sharing it with another woman, a woman that didn't care about me or better herself. She was willing to hop in bed with a married man regardless of the consequences."

She was right…Mallory didn't care about his marriage, if any she wanted him to herself…like a reminder of his past.

Drew knew that most married men swooped down on lonely and desperate women. They were the easy prey for a quick lay. Women who would spend all day and night daydreaming about a wonderful, thoughtful, and supportive man that they would put everything moral and right on the back burners for him. There were so many women who just needed to hear, "You're beautiful," "You have a great personality," "If I was your man, you'll want for nothing." Most married men, Drew included, gave these women false hopes of a committed relationship. Instead of building these women's self-esteem up, they tore it down with the final blow of staying with their wives.

"Janice, you can trust me again. I'll be here at home…no more late nights out."

"If I agree to this, what about your baby and *her*. How would I fit into this split family?" A tear slowly crept out Janice's eye.

"You are and will always be first in my life, Janice. I hope you will accept the baby and help me raise him or her.

Janice pushed away from the table and slapped Drew.

"What the hell is wrong with you?" Drew grabbed his stinging face.

"I can't do this, Drew…not right now…I just can't…I can't accept that woman's child."

"I don't know what to say, Janice. I love you. Can you think about it please—"

"It's time for you to go. This is too much for me. I need time to think. No promise. I just can't get over what you have done to us."

CHAPTER 18

Alison

"That was nice, wasn't it, Chantay. I loved the roof top patio, what about you?"

"Lovely I say. I can't wait for the photo shoot to be over so we can shop at the Eaton Centre."

The two of them sat chitchatting about clothes, music, and men. Alison missed Alan. They never went days without speaking and now, because of her betrayal, a week has gone by. 'Was he that upset?' her thoughts bounced around.

"Okay, Alison, let's do some more stills here by the garden, change clothes and shoot inside. It'll be a wrap soon my dear. François the photographer gleamed.

Casa Loma in Toronto was beautiful. The stained-glass dome lined the sixty-foot ceiling in the great hall. A library and billiard room were a meniscal of amenities. Formal and informal gardens, surrounded the castle.

"Do you want me here?" She pointed to a bloom of bright colorful flowers.

"Exactly. Let's try you kneeling to smell the flowers…and take your hand to cupped a few." His fingers snapped twice.

Alison gracefully abided in François instructions. Although her mind lingered elsewhere. She had to focus on work. Alan would not be a part of it.

"Alison, dear, a few shots of you walking away. As you're walking, I want you to glance over shoulder looking down…hmm…sad, but not too sad."

'That shouldn't be too hard' the words idled in her mind.

"Perfect! That's what I wanted. Solemn. You had sadness, but your dignity still shone through. Brave and strong."

François had redeemed her with those words. She was no longer going to sit and be sad. Why should she. She had a choice in this family matter as much as Alan and she wasn't going to back down because his feelings were hurt.

"Thank you, François." She smiled. "Thank you."

"Get changed and I'll meet you inside."

Her stomach quivered as she tapped on Alan's name to call. Nothing. Quickly, she scrolled through her contact list. She waited, then pushed Tonya's name. Again, nothing. She opted not to leave a message.

With her renewed spirit, Alison, was on top of the world and wasn't going to let nothing or no one bring her down.

"Okay, Alison, I want you to hold the left side of the dress up and lean against that enormous dining table. I want to capture the Circassian walnut panels for the background," François instructed.

She stretched her leg and on the ball of foot she arched it. Pulling the fiery red semi-sheer long dress up to her thigh. Alison head slowly lay back turned toward François; she gave a slight pucker of red lips. Click, click, and click the camera sang. After a few shots, Alison rushed to put on another outfit. This time it was a white satin lingerie. The bust line dipped to her stomach and rested slightly off shoulders. Lights and fans sat positioned. Alison sprawled across a Victorian bed, an oversized pillow placed under her head and rose petals covering her partially naked body. For an overhead shot, François steadied himself atop a ladder.

"Lay on your side Alison and bring your right leg slightly over the left…good." He stepped down a little. "Now lean forward a little, tilt your head down and look up with your eyes…yes…that's it. Give me a wink."

She felt sexy and powerful.

"Guess what my dear? We are done. Go enjoy the rest of your freaking day." François, again, snapped his fingers twice.

Looking at Chantay, "Thank God this is over. I'm starving and I want to get some rest."

"I'm with you on that. We can shop tomorrow. We won't have that long though. Our planes leave for Barcelona early afternoon." Chantay huffed.

The women spent the rest of their evening relaxing in the luxurious spa scented with lavender and jasmine. They sipped herbal teas and enjoyed a full body massage. They dressed in comfortable khaki pants, over-sized t-shirts, and flip flops. Strolling through the elegant hotel, laughing, they stopped in a souvenir shop.

"Chantay, you really like doing hair, don't you?"

With a quizzical look Chantay spoke, "Of course I do. You know that. You already know I had to work hard to get to this point in life."

"I know you did. I admire how you put your career first." Alison picked up a miniature sculpture of Niagara Falls.

"When I started out, clients didn't appreciate a damn thing." Chantay hissed reliving her past.

"I know what you mean…I mean unappreciated slobs."

Both laughed.

"Alison, I worked ten hours a day and maybe more standing on my feet and these non-appreciative women complain about the smallest thing. 'Oh, you didn't wash it good enough,' 'Those curlers are not hot enough' or my best one, 'I don't tip because you stylist charge too much.' Isn't it a shame they know we have to charge to pay for our products and time."

"Girl, I know all that complaining got to you."

"Oh, wait, Alison, that booth rental the shop owners charged was crazy high."

"I'm glad you got into this business Chantay. I wouldn't know who could style my hair better than you. In the past, my hair was a mess. I didn't really agree with the last stylist; she just couldn't do the job. I took Vivica A. Fox's theory—I hired someone who knows black hair and should be compensated for it. There's too many of us black folks out here whose talent go by the wayside because we're not given a chance."

"I agree with you Alison, but stylist have to love what they do and respect their clients."

When they arrived back in the room. Alison sat on her bed glanced around the room. Her career is first. Alan need to understand that she mumbled. She loved him, but couldn't see herself being a mom right now. She wanted to travel with her husband. She wanted to have quiet moments. Their careers took so much of their time and a baby right now would only add to it. If only Alan could wait a few more years and she may be ready. She slipped the khakis and flip-flops off and lay on the bed in her bra and panties. Alison let the sleep take hold.

CHAPTER 19

Alan

A late Saturday night and Alan was enjoying a sports drink and watching a thriller on HBO. For the two weeks Alison had been gone, he tried to forget the last conversation they had. He didn't want to be reminded how cold she sounded towards him. He did love her, and hoped she would have a change of heart. 'They would talk when she got home' he reminded himself.

He extended the olive branch and called Alison, to pick her up from the airport. Instead, she simply sent him a text refusing the ride.

Keys, jarred Alan from the tv. Slowly, he walked towards the foyer. Standing by the staircase, was Alison. He wanted to embrace her, the more he studied her face, Alan chose to tread carefully.

His voice was faint. "Hey baby."

Dryly, Alison spoke. "Hey."

"Let me get those." He reached for her bags.

Alan tucked a bag under his arm and with each hand picked up two larger suitcases on wheels. He jogged up the staircase with Alison strutting behind.

Placing the luggage in the closet Alan stood in front of Alison. "Babe, we need to talk." He reached for her.

"Alan, I'm really tired can this wait?" She pushed away from him.

"We're going to talk about this Alison and you're not going to slither you way out of it."

"Fine." She huffed. "I'm going to take a shower. Unless you want to come in there and talk, I'll be out in little."

"Take your shower."

Alan remembered the tv was still on in the family room. Trotting down the rear staircase leading to the kitchen, he reached the family room. The movie still playing, he sat down and got comfortable. "What the fuck." He yelled at the tv. The actors running for their life through foggy forest leaving behind an empty cabin. A man with a hockey mask and machete took long steps behind them.

A muffled ringing and vibration startled him. He reached into the jean pocket and pulled out his cellphone.

"Hello." He whispered.

"Alan is this a good time to talk?"

"Tonya. It's late and Alison is back."

"Oh wow. I'm sorry. Quick question. Can you come over tomorrow? I need help with getting Asia's new bed set together."

"Tomorrow?" Alan breathed heavily. "I...I don't know Tonya. Alison and I...well, we need to talk about something. I'm not sure if I would be able to help."

"Is everything okay with you and Alison?"

"We just need to clear something up."

"I get it. Um, I'll appreciate if you can come, but don't worry about it. Have a good night okay."

Two weeks ago, he had Tonya sitting on the sofa right here in the family room. Both a little intoxicated in close proximity staring into each other eyes. He wanted her and knew she wanted him. His hand had trailed Tonya's bare arm up to her neck. His fingers gripped her soft hair. Gently their foreheads met each other. His nose to hers. His lips to hers. At that moment, Alan had realized he crossed the line. He took Tonya home.

Alan shook the memory away and headed back upstairs. Once at the bedroom door, he watched Alison sleeping peacefully. He stood there minutes more and wondered was it really necessary to have a baby? Was he wrong to be so upset at his wife? Should he give in?

***

Morning dew rested on the windows. Alan had finished his workout routine. Gulping down water, he jogged up the stairs. Back in the bedroom Alison still slept peacefully. He peeled off the wet shorts and tank top, then pulled the ankle black socks off. He leaned into the mirror taking a closer look at the fine shadow of hair forming its goatee cut. Lifting his arms, he sniffed, shook his head, and frowned. "Whew." He laughed.

He stepped out of the boxer briefs and with his manhood hanging and glistening from the sweat, Alan stepped into the shower. The hot water sprayed from atop and front. He sang, while lathering with his sport scent body wash. He took the wash cloth under his arms, chest, around and under his manhood. Ringing the washcloth, he lathered it again and took it between his butt cheeks. His body was rinsed with the hot water. Another washcloth Alan wet it and washed his face.

He wrapped a plush towel around his waist and stepped onto the waiting rug. Just then Alison appeared.

"Good morning." He sang to her.

Hers was flat. "Good morning."

"So, babe, can we talk now?"

"Alan, I just got up. Can you give me a moment? Geez."

Alan was dumbfounded. Alison had been stand-offish since she got home last night.

"Whatever, Alison, I'll be downstairs."

"No, Alan, let's talk, right now."

Cautiously, he moved slowly toward her. Taking her hand, he led her to the chaise and sat next to her.

"Alison, I'm sorry for not answering your calls when you were away. I was upset and hurt baby…"

"So, you can be upset and hurt and act like a damn child. I could've been hurt or something."

"But you weren't Alison. If something was wrong, I'm sure you would've left a message. Anyway, can you tell me why you don't want a baby…with me?"

"With you?" She jerked her head. "I don't want a baby with anyone right now. Alan, I like our lives how it is. I enjoy the freedom. A baby will slow that down."

"A baby won't slow us down; it'll change us into a family. A family that will do things together. Make memories. I want to be a father, baby, with you doing your little mother thing." He tickled her side.

"Alan please stop. I'm very serious. Right now, isn't the time. Come on, our careers are going great—"

"If not now, when?" Now standing he looked down at her. "We're not getting any younger."

Alison stood. "Sweetheart." She held the sides of his face. "I…I don't want kids. I'm sorry I hadn't said so earlier on. I mean at first, I did, but something changed. Life happened."

"What does that even mean Alison?"

"I don't know Alan. Maybe, I'll rethink this, but not now."

The feeling he had when he caught her taking that pill, had returned, but worse. He sat on the chaise and she disappeared into the bathroom.

Alan reached for his cellphone.

"I'll be over in an hour."

CHAPTER 20

Alan

"Daryl, get your tools and come help me at Tonya's."

"Wait, you're going to see that gorgeous little thing?" Daryl hollered.

"Calm down, man. She asked me to help with assembling her daughter's bedroom set. I want you to help, so get your tools and I'll text you the address."

With the windows lowered, the warm and breezy wind circled his exposed arms. A Mary J. Blige song blared from his iPhone through the Bose speakers. Alison words played in his mind. He didn't want to wait until she figured it out, if ever. The hot Atlanta sun beamed rays into his covered eyes. Alan peeked into the rearview mirror, admiring his Ray-Bans. His head bobbed to another Mary's hit, *Mr. Wrong.* Another ten minutes he saw his exit.

"I thought you weren't coming, Alan, I was getting worried." Tonya took him by the arm and led him down a long hallway filled with black arts. He studied each one. He never knew Tonya was an art collector, especially of black art. Alan stopped at an art piece by Henry Rios Battle, 'Midnight Snack.' A man and woman sat on an elegant bed, the woman dressed in a gold negligee and a tray of different fruits beside her and the man positioned behind her.

"You like that one, huh?" Tonya stood behind Alan.

"Yeah, it's nice, you know, romantic."

"I love romantic interludes. Look at this one." Tonya put her arms around Alan and turned him to the opposite wall. "this one is called 'Always and Forever.' See how the woman is lying back and he's over her about to plant a kiss?" Tonya winked. "I love the foreplay and anticipation of love itself."

"Is that so?" Alan admired the glow in her eyes.

Tonya placed both hands on Alan's firm face and slowly moved her hands downward. She traced the outline of his lips neatly trimmed by his goatee.

Alan's breath became short as he allowed her to continue to seduce him. It was wrong, but could not hurt as long as it did not go any further.

"Alan, I want you." Tonya squeezed him through nylon shorts. Pushing him against the wall, she indulged him with wet kisses.

"Come on, Tonya stop…" He barely spoke.

"Do you want me too, really?" She continued to squeeze him.

"I mean, where's Asia she might see us."

"How thoughtful of you, but Asia isn't here. She's next door at a sleepover."

Saved by the bell he was. "Tonya," he pushed her away. "Someone's at your door, maybe it's Daryl."

"Daryl, why is he here?"

"I asked him to bring some tools and help me."

Tonya straightened her clothes and sashayed to the door.

Daryl walked in with a toolbox tucked under his left arm.

"What the hell do you have on, Daryl?" Alan questioned.

"I came prepared. You don't like my pinstriped overall suit. I'm a hard-working man. Tell him, Tonya."

Tonya walked over and kissed him on the lips.

Daryl's toothy grin widened. "What was that for?"

"I thought that a hardworking man deserves a kiss, you know what I mean, Alan." Tonya winked at him.

"Show us what you need done." Alan pivoted.

They walked down the hallway where Alan admired the artwork and got a taste of the vixen. Tonya showed them what needed to be assembled and left the men alone.

"Alan, what's going on? What did I walk into?"

"She came onto me. I mean, we were about to get busy."

"Oh snap!" Daryl raised his hand for a high-five. "Shit man, you want me to leave? We can put this damn bed together later."

"Naw, let's just do this so I can go home." Alan had begun to separate pieces.

"Wait, hold up…you telling me you don't want to hit that. I know you do."

"Here's the deal Daryl, I know she kissed you to see how I was going to react and I'll admit I was a little angry, but come on, man, I can't do this."

"You worried about Alison, huh?"

Alan ripped plastic casing away from the wood furniture. "Daryl, Alison don't want to have kids."

"She doesn't want to have sex with you anymore?"

Alan stopped ripping the plastic. "Daryl is your mind always on sex? I'm sure she wants the sex, but she doesn't want a baby from it. I caught her a few weeks ago still taking the pill…"

"That's why you came out that night…to the club and little fine missy here showed up. Hey what happened when I dropped you two at your house." Daryl now, fully engaged to Alan.

"Nothing happened."

"Nothing?"

"I was mad as hell with Alison that night and then Tonya was right there, so close, I could smell her sweetness. I wanted to, but I couldn't."

"When the last time you had some?"

"Sex?"

"Yes, Alan, sex."

"Before Alison left.

Daryl reached into his farmer John outfit and pulled out two large ribbed condoms. "I carry these like my American Express card. Never leave home without them. Take one man and let yourself have some fun. We will put this set together quick and I'll leave. She wants it…you give it to her like she never fucking had it."

Alan reluctantly put the condom in his pocket.

"You the man." Daryl hit Alan on the back.

Hours went by and the two men finally had the bedroom set assembled. After a glass of lemonade, Daryl gathered his toolbox and left.

"Call me as soon as you get the time." Daryl winked at Alan. "I'll see you later, little lady, and thanks for the kiss." He pecked Tonya on the cheek.

As soon as Tonya shut the door, time stood still. Alan could hear his heart beating. His watch read 1p.m. He had been gone six hours.

"Alan, come here." Tonya reached for his hand. "I think you should go; this isn't the right time. I was wrong to come on to you like that. One thing I don't want to get into any trouble with Alison." She gave him a friendly hug, extending her body away from him.

Alan pointed to the sofa. "May I sit down for a minute?"

"What's on your mind?"

"I know what I'm feeling isn't right. I want you too, but I just don't see it happening…"

"Not at all…what about—"

Alan placed his finger over Tonya lips. "Not now. If this happens let it, don't force it." He stroked her short bob hairstyle.

"Alan Perry, that's why I like you so much…you're a gentleman and very caring. I hope Alison realizes she has a good man and a fine one at that. If you were my husband, I would sex you every minute I had. Your dinner will be ready every night and a hot shower waiting for you when you got home. Anything you wanted to do to me you could do." She licked her lips.

"Thanks, Tonya. Hey, enough talk about me. Why don't you have someone special in your life?"

Tonya huffed then moved from the sofa. With her hands on her hips, she walked to the bay window. She began to speak softly with her back still to Alan. "I loved Eric, Asia's father, but he had other plans."

"Were you guys together for a while?" Alan now stood behind her.

Outside, the wind swayed the tree branches. Asia rode past on a tricycle with her neighbor.

"Yeah, we were together for a long time. He promised me everything, cars, diamonds, a nice home, and of course the ring. I did everything for him then one day he got it in his mind to…" Tonya sniffled and wiped tears, "hit me."

"He did what! That punk ass bitch."

"Don't be too hard on him, Alan. I know I made him do it most of the time."

"Are you kidding? He is a grown man and makes his own choices. Don't blame yourself for this." Alan pulled Tonya close.

"When I became pregnant with Asia he totally changed. A couple of times he would beat me, but not enough to leave bruises. Oh, he was smart. I think he wanted me to lose the baby, but I begged him to stop. He came up with a wild plan that it was better for him to leave for a while and get himself together so he joined the Air Force. I thought that was a good idea until he came after Asia was born and said he didn't want us."

"I'm sorry for that. You did not deserve what happened. How could he walk away from a beautiful woman and his child? I love Asia, she adorable. I just can't believe a man could do that."

"Alan, all men aren't alike. I told Alison about him, but she sort of took his side."

"Not Alison. You may have misunderstood her."

"Maybe, but I needed a friend and that's why I confessed all this to her. I could tell she's as caring as you and I really like her despite, how I feel for you."

Alan put his arm around her shoulder and whispered, "I like you too."

CHAPTER 21

Alison

The sun's hues changed from yellow to orange as the hours passed by. Alison had not heard from her husband all day. He never left without saying where he was going. But then again, they never had a fight quite like this one. She desperately wanted to feel her husband arms around her and she was going to make all attempts to get it.

"Hey girl. How are you?"

"Alison, wow, I didn't expect to hear from you today." Tonya calmly and slowly said.

"Really. Why is that? I got home late last night and girl I was tired."

"The last time I saw you, I was a mess. Crying and over the top about Eric—"

Alison laughed. "You mean when you broke down in the garden scaring my fish?" She cleared her throat. "Tonya, don't worry about him. You have so much more to give. Don't let that fool smolder your light."

"I know and I appreciate that."

"And we all definitely have problems…hey, you want to come over for a little?"

"I told Alan that I wanted to stop by."

"When did you talk to him?"

"A little while ago. He and Daryl came by to assemble Asia's bedroom set."

Hit by a bomb. Alison flopped down on the chaise. She felt waves move through her stomach. Can't sit, she hurriedly walked to the bedroom patio door. She breathed the fresh air and calmed her emotions.

"Is he still there?"

"Oh, no, he left maybe one or two hours ago."

"He left with Daryl?"

"Alison, Daryl had already left. I asked Alan to stay just for a little to talk. I told him about Eric."

Alison felt some kind of way. "So, are you coming or what?"

"I guess. Yeah. Girls night. I'll be there."

***

Alison tidied the family room and made an artichoke dip. She changed into blue jeans, pink t-shirt, and flip-flops. Music flowing from the speakers, Alison did her best karaoke performance.

She dipped her head and shook it side to side. Closing her eyes, she let the music fill her soul. She wrapped her arms around herself and rocked her body. She continued singing until…

"Baby, you sound good—"

Quickly, she turned around. "Alan. You scared me. How long you've been standing there?"

"Long enough to see that you seem happy. Alison, I love you."

"I love you too." She paused the music. "I am so sorry about this morning. We will figure this out, I promise…"

"To be honest, Alison, you have to figure it out. I am here waiting on you."

"Alan." She sang the words. "Please, please be patient with me. Right now, baby, this moment we have each other. And tomorrow we wake up, we have each other. Who knows I may have a different view tomorrow? Just be patient with me." She stood on her toes and kissed him. Seeing that he didn't move, her arms locked around him. Feverishly, she kissed him again. Her tongue circled his lips. She felt his hands move the length of her back. She pushed into him more.

The couple embraced more. The gate intercom buzzed.

"Ah, come on. Who is it?" Alan moaned.

Alison cleared her throat. "It should be Tonya. I invited her over."

"You…you did why?"

"Thought it would be cool for her to come hang out and besides, I wanted to ask you two something."

Alison skipped through the kitchen into the foyer. She looked herself over in the mirror.

"Come on in, Tonya."

She waved for Tonya to follow her. They stopped in the kitchen and Alison set three glasses on the counter. She removed the dip from the fridge and handed it to Tonya while she grabbed the glasses and pitcher of ice-tea. When they returned to the family room, Alan had changed the music to Phil Collins' *In the Air* and lay back on the leather love seat.

Tonya stopped suddenly when she saw Alan and Alison almost tripped over her.

"Girl, what's wrong. You act like you seen a ghost."

"I didn't expect to see Alan."

"Why not? He lives here. You see me holding three glasses don't you." Alison look between the two. "Alan, get up and help us."

"Thanks, Alan." Tonya said as she let the bowl of dip pass into his hands.

"Alison, I was a little surprised because when you asked me to come over, I thought it was going to be a girl's night. You know what I mean." Tonya danced.

"I have an idea I want to run by you and Alan."

Tonya and Alan looked at each other.

"Let's have a '70's themed party. Right here by the pool. Every guest has to come dressed to impress. We must have '70's music, games, and food. You know a table for bid wiz and spades." Alison was excited, moving from seat to seat. "So, what do you guys think?"

Alan eyes widened. "I think it's a good idea. We can do this."

"Well, Tonya?"

Tonya waved her hands in the air. "Let's do it, it'll be fun. I can't wait to do the bump, that's such a simple dance…ooh I know exactly how I want my hair and the clothes…"

"Hold on girlfriend don't spill your beans yet. What we need to do is plan this out and set a date. I'm pretty open with my schedule for a moment, but we'll work around Alan's."

Ten o'clock had come and three of them finally mapped out their big party. Alison felt excited.

"Okay, people." Tonya stood. "I know you want to be alone and I need to check on Asia. My neighbors will let her stay up all night. They don't have any bed time rules for their daughter." Her voice dry.

"Asia is with your neighbors? Isn't she sort of young to stay over with someone?" Alison asked.

"I trust them. I've known them since Asia was a baby. After Eric left us, I moved next door to the Williams and they have really been a big help to me. Their daughter is Asia's age they're good people.

"I would be concerned, but since you explained your relationship with your neighbors, I guess that's okay. Who am I to say anything?"

"It's time for me to go and I had fun. This party is going to be the bomb. Oh, we can't forget to invite Daryl. I would love to see what he would wear. Alan, remember that outfit he had on this morning?"

They both laughed.

"I guess Daryl gave you all something to laugh at, huh?" Alison tried to laugh, but as phony as it was to her, they had to know it too.

"Yeah, he did, he looked like farmer John, but Daryl is so cute it doesn't matter what he wear he still looks good." Tonya blushed.

Alison smiled while Alan's lips turned down and he stared hard and long at Tonya.

"Tonya, I know you're ready to go, but I have one question…have you finally went out with him?" Alison clasped her hands together.

"With Daryl uh, no, not yet."

"We'll talk about it later. Give Asia a kiss for us when she comes home."

Alan escorted Tonya to the door and watched her safely to the car.

When he returned to the family room, music echoed softly in the dimly lit room. Alison sat nearby.

With her hand extended, "Alan come, sit next to me."

"Why on earth do you want to have this party?" He caressed her thigh.

"Why not? Something fun to do. Don't you get tired of the same things. You know we have to go with the flow and fun."

"Oh, I don't mind. I was surprised you thought of this now when…how we are?" His eyes lovingly stared at hers.

"I wanted to start making up to you figured a party…" she pumped her hands in the air. "Would be good. And, this…"

Alison pulled Alan on top of her. She kissed him passionately allowing her tongue to slowly enter his mouth. She wrapped her legs around his back and pushed her hips up to him.

Alan sat up removed his top then shorts. Alison kneeled before him and used her teeth to grip the boxer briefs. She slowly pulled the briefs down, stopping mid-section to take in Alan's scent. She grabbed his butt, pulled him closer and twirled her head around in his groin. She gripped the briefs again with her teeth and continued downward.

With wet slippery licks, Alison moved along his muscular leg while massaging him. She nibbled on his thighs with a bite here and there. He moaned with pleasure. She let her tongue play with his almost hidden navel. Alison moved back to his excitement and took him in completely. She moaned feeling her husband deep in her.

Bringing Alan to the point of climax Alison stopped. "Alan, do me."

Alan grabbed the quilt, placed it on the floor, and lay Alison on it. He quickly and gently gave her what she desperately long for.

CHAPTER 22

Drew

Drew sat on the sofa and listened to Tim explain all his illness again as if Drew was to magically find a cure. Drew was more concerned with his own situation and didn't want to hear Tim babble.

He had talked to Janice numerous times since their last dinner and tried each time to convince her to take him back and it would be better. Each time Janice ended the call with a shallow, "I don't know."

Four months had passed since she put him out and four months of celibacy for him. He gave up women to be with the one he loved...Janice. To live in a tempted world, Drew didn't know how long he'd survive.

"Drew, did you hear me? I'm going to tell Alison about me."

"I don't care. You should've told her a long time ago. Why didn't you?"

"Don't know. Guess I didn't want to freak her out. I need her. She's really a good person and I don't want to lose her."

"You don't have to tell me about her. I know all too well."

They sat by the window watching fierce rain and hail from the heavens. New York was under a severe thunderstorm, with high winds.

"I haven't spoken to Alison in a while, have you?" Tim sipped on a chardonnay.

"Actually, she called me a couple of weeks ago. She was having some issues with that pretty boy husband of hers. He was hanging around with one of her friends." Drew never turned from the window.

"Really? She briefly mentioned some woman when she was here."

Drew scratched between his legs. "She was wondering all types of shit man. You know, like if a man cheat, why…I told her it can happen."

"Sounds like you and Alison have rekindled some old feelings."

"Nothing like that. I told her what happened, asked for her forgiveness, and we're cool."

Drew fidgeted with his shirt and rubbed the bristle hairs that pinched their way through his chin. He crossed his arms and turned his attention back to the window.

"Drew, what's on your mind. You have been staring out that damn window too long. Have a beer or something, shit, you're making me nervous."

"I can't do this anymore, Tim. What's the fucking use trying to be a faithful man if I don't have to be?"

"What are you saying? I hope you're not about to do something crazy."

"I've been begging Janice for months to let me come home and all she can say is 'I don't know.' Fuck a *I don't know.* I am her husband. Drew stood with arms stretched out onto the window. The window took a hazy covering from his breath. "I have not had sex in four fucking months, Tim, four. My balls are probably beyond blue."

"You better go take care of that…right there in the bathroom." He pointed.

Drew grabbed his pants and shook his manhood up and down. I don't need to when I can get it the natural good way. Besides that'll only make me want it more." As a revelation came to him. "It's not cheating if I get if from Mallory."

"Okay, you *have* lost your mind. You're trying to get mixed up with that crazy broad again?"

Hail pounding the window and the rustling of high winds crept through the silence. Neither said a word. Drew dragged his feet as he pulled a beer from the fridge. Tim looked over his shoulder.

"Should it matter? We're having a child together and my own wife can't make up her mind."

"Drew, think about what you're saying. You told Janice that you wanted to change, but if she finds out that you went back to Mallory…you're asking for a divorce for sure."

"Why are you so righteous, Tim, huh, why?"

Tim looked down then sipped his drink. "I'm not righteous, but I try to be a gentleman and understand. Women love it when we men can understand them, you know, get in tune with their feelings."

"In-tune my ass, you gay bitch."

Both laughed.

"Hey, you know I'm far from that shit. I'm just a good old-fashion caring guy. Maybe if there was more of me out there a whole lot of women would be happy."

"Whatever, man, I made a decision. I'm moving out soon. I really appreciate your hospitality, good old-fashion man, but I need to be on my own. I need to sort things out."

"Come on, man, you can stay here as long as you need to…'

Thanks Tim, but I need to do this…I need privacy."

"You the boss and look I'm going to take a walk. I need to get some air."

"In this storm?"

"The storm will pass. A little water ain't going to hurt especially what I have. I'm going to call Alison when I get back."

Tim removed his black leather jacket from the wall hook. He grabbed his black-fitted baseball cap and left.

***

Drew made an over-roasted turkey sandwich on wheat bread with miracle whip. Crunchy Cheetos surrounded the sandwich on an oval plate. He took an ice-cold beer from the fridge and went to the guest room. He called home for the last four months. He sat on the bed with the plate on his lap and beer on the nightstand. The day had become night and the storm subsided.

His cell phone vibrated. He was shocked to see who was calling.

"Hey what's up?" he said in a smooth voice.

"I was thinking about you. I wanted to talk."

"Really, I was thinking about you too. Actually, I mentioned you tonight."

"Wow, this must be something. What did you say about me?"

Drew was lost for words. "That I wanted to see you. It's been a while since we actually sat down and looked at each other without fighting or worried about the situation."

"You're right I should've called a long time ago. Will you come over?"

"I'll be there in forty-five minutes." He put the cell away, hurried to the kitchen, wiped the plate out, and put the empty bottle in the trash. Never before had he been so anxious, but for her to call was a sign of good things to come. Drew took a five-minute shower, splashed on Jean Paul Gautier cologne, brushed his teeth, and gargled with mint mouthwash. This may be a lucky night for him and he was ready.

He stopped at the corner florist, picked out roses and a *National Enquirer Magazine* just in case the night didn't go as expected, he could use the cheesy paper for conversation.

He drove south on Fifth Street passing Central Park. On occasional stops at red lights, Drew flipped through the paper. He was about to pull off when he saw a familiar face. He pulled the car over and turned the overhead light on. It couldn't be. He laughed then felt complete sadness. Had Alison seen the pictures. How could Alan be so thoughtless to be caught up in something like this? He wanted to call Alison, but tonight he needed to get to his destination without distractions.

He'd call her later. He sped out the parking spot. When he reached his destination, he sat in the car. Was this the right thing to do? He would make it the right thing. He smiled and stepped out the car.

He grabbed the roses, paper, and turned off his cell phone. Tonight, he wanted no distractions for it had been too long and his manhood was ready.

"Come on in, Drew."

"What's up, Mallory?" Drew Kicked the door shut.

CHAPTER 23

Tim

Tim had the place to himself for the weekend. Drew didn't come back until Monday evening after work. He didn't say where he went nor did Tim ask. Tim was glad to get home. He was tired and his body ached. All day at work he tossed the idea of calling Alison. No matter the outcome he would respect her decision. Time to face the loaded gun and pull the trigger.

"Baby girl, what's been going on?" His voice deep and sultry.

"Tim, so much has been happening I don't know how to begin."

"Take your time, baby, and just let it out one at a time."

When his turn came would he be so confident? Silence swept across the phone. He looked out the window the sun illuminated orange and red hues across the eastern sky.

"Alison, are you okay?"

"No. Alan caught me taking my birth control pills and he was pissed."

"I thought you two talked about having kids, what happened?"

"We did talk about it...I wasn't completely honest with him on my view—"

Tim body rested on the sofa, one leg stretched, the other on top. "There should be no secrets Alison, you know that."

"I shouldn't have secrets?" She sniffed and snorted. "He's in the tabloids with some naked women all over him!"

"What? Tabloid. Women."

Tim let Alison vent for the next hour before saying a word. Her voice made him feel relaxed and sure.

"Alison, I have something to tell you. I wasn't honest what happened with Felicia. I want you to brace yourself and I understand if you don't want to talk to me again—"

"Stop babbling Tim and tell me."

"I didn't tell you before because—"

"Tim!"

"I'm HIV positive, Alison."

Silence. A lump formed in his throat and he swallowed hard.

"Alison, say something."

"I-I don't know what to say…I'm sorry."

"Do you hate me?"

"Why would I hate you? You're my friend, how did this happen?"

He sighed and told Alison of Felicia's blood transfusion and they didn't find out until it was too late for either of them.

"Tim! I can't lose you. Are you on any medication or something?"

He snickered a little. "I don't plan on going anywhere, baby girl. I am on meds. I take one day at a time."

"Is there anything, I mean anything I can do?"

"Just be my friend."

"I'm here for you, always."

He cleared his throat. "Alison, I'm going to be all right. As long as I know I have you in my life, if it's only as friends. You know I always loved you, right?"

"Of course, I knew…you remember the words I sung to you?"

"I heard every word, but I couldn't act on them. Alison, you're a very special person not only to me, but so many people. Your husband is a lucky man and I hope he knows that."

"I hope he does."

CHAPTER 24

Alison

"How could you be so irresponsible, Alan, huh?" She pushed him.

"Keep your hands off me, Alison. I don't know where you got that from, but I don't play that."

"Oh, what you going to do, hit me?" She drew back her fists.

"No, Alison, I'm not, as a matter of fact we won't have this conversation until you calm down." Hastily, Alan walked into the family room.

Alison didn't want to argue with him, but she wanted answers. "Alan, I apologize for putting my hands on you. Tell me what happened."

"For the last time…Daryl and I went to this party, a bunch of women…lesbians, were there and I don't remember what happened. They drugged us."

"Why were you even there in the first place? And you're telling me, lesbians, women that like women, drugged you two. Why, Alan, why would they want to do that?"

"Does it matter, Alison, really? I was out with my boys and Daryl and I decided to go see what the party was all about." Alan disappeared towards the kitchen.

Hot on his heels, Alison followed. "I don't understand why you even stayed once you got to this so-called party. If that was me I would've—"

"Well, it wasn't you and I stayed. You act like I slept with them."

"These pictures suggest otherwise, Alan." She shook them at him. "Do you see what I see—you and Daryl stupid behinds laid back with your underwear down and nasty, stank, whores sitting on your laps. Wow! I don't know what to do about you?"

"You talk like I'm a child. I don't know what's gotten into you."

"This is all you. You did this. Don't turn this on me—"

"You know what I think…ever since Tonya started coming over your attitude has changed. You act like you hate the girl, then love her. What has she done to you? Furthermore, you stop trusting me."

Part of her believed something wasn't right with Alan's sudden interest with Tonya and he was in the wrong to ignore her concerns. Was he tired of the day-in day-out routine of marriage? Was he still hurting about the baby issue?

"What's happening to us Alan?"

"Like I said, you stopped trusting me. I'm going to pick up the rest of party things."

"You're going to go through with it after all this? I mean, what will people say about those pictures and you and Daryl suspended?"

"I really don't feel like having it, but since we already committed ourselves, hey, why the fuck not. And who gives a fuck what people will say. Don't care! Don't fucking care!" He took a swallow from the bottled water, grabbed his keys, fleece jacket, and left without uttering another word.

With all the badgering she had done Alison forgot to tell him about Tim. Maybe if Alan knew he would've been a little more polite. How thoughtless for her to use Tim's health for her sympathy. She sank to a new low. Shame.

***

Alison knew not telling Alan about this was going to add fuel to the fire. He would want to be there for her no matter what they were going through. Enough was enough, she was going crazy and wanted help.

A young girl, beautiful chestnut brown skin and green eyes, sat behind a glass desk. "May I help you?"

"I have a 2:00 p.m. appointment with Dr. Rios." Fidgeting with her purse, Alison spoke.

"Mrs. Perry. Okay, I have you right here." The receptionist clicked a few times with the computer mouse. "Have a seat and fill out this questionnaire and someone would be with you shortly." She smiled handing Alison a clipboard.

With her baseball cap pulled down, Alison, took a corner seat. Plopping down on the plush chair, she exhaled. Question one, you felt much more self-confident than usual? Yes, she checked. She whispered, "I am confident." Question two, you were irritable or shouted at people? Yes, she checked. A few more questions she continued to check the boxes.

"Mrs. Perry?" A tall lady, with a navy-blue pencil skirt and white blouse appeared at the door.

Alison lifted her hand, quickly gathered her belongings, and followed the woman. The hallway insulated with a tan-colored carpet was accented by light gold walls and white borders.

"Have a seat in here the woman extended her arm."

Planters held big green leafy plants in two corners of the office. Behind the oak desk, a large picture window gave view to trees, green and red shrubs, and water sprouting from a fountain. Alison felt quite relaxed.

Taking a seat at the desk Alison placed her belongings in an empty chair. She watched the tall lady smoothly sit.

A beautiful smile, perfectly white straight teeth the woman spoke. "I'm Doctor Rios-Psychologist." She scribbled on a note pad. "I want you to know, feel comfortable to share any information. Our meetings are confidential."

Alison nodded.

"Okay. May I have the clipboard. Let's see what you've checked."

Alison did as requested. "Um, doctor, I don't know why I'm here." She looked beyond the doctor and fixated on the fountain.

Sighing, the doctor said, "I'm not here to judge you. And remember whatever you tell me is confidential. We're going to talk. Tell me what's been going on. Why *did* you come here today?"

"My husband and I seem to argue…well not argue, but disagree on a lot…well, not on lot—"

"It's okay Alison we can take this slow. I see on your questionnaire you've checked off items that can indicate there may be mood swings, irritability, highly motivated…energized at times. These can be signs of Bipolar." She placed her hands palm down on the papers.

Alison twirled strands of her hair beneath the baseball cap. "Really?" Alison closed her eyes and shook her head. Great, another thing to freaking stress me out." She huffed.

"Stress you out?" The doctor started writing.

"Yes. Besides the fact my husband wants a baby and I don't, now this…I may be bipolar." Her eyes went up.

"So, your husband wants a baby and you don't. Why don't you?"

Alison's shoulders inched up and down. "I don't know." She sat forward. "I like it the way it is, Alan and I. I mean my career is going well…I don't want to pause that yet."

The doctor continued writing. "I understand." She took her glasses off. "You mentioned having a baby was one of the issues. What are the other issues?"

"I'm not happy with my husband's friendship with a mutual female friend and he has been suspended from the league for doing ignorant stuff." She tapped her forefinger on the desk.

"Have you spoken to your husband about these things?"

She laughed. "Have I? He knows, he just doesn't listen."

"Hmm…" the doctor looked at Alison. "Have you sat down with him and shared what's on your mind? About the baby, the friend, his suspension? Without yelling and accusing?"

Alison looked away. "He should know."

Doctor Rios stood, folded her arms, and watched birds looping around the fountain. "Alison, can you go into detail about what you wrote on the questionnaire. You put rape, in the section marked other."

She lay back in the chair and lifted her cap slightly. "It happened early on in my career. I was having a photo session and this photographer-Diane, tried to rape me." Alison exhaled. I can remember her hands, not smooth and soft like a woman, but rough. She touched me on my breasts and rested her large body on me. So many things happened at that moment, but I remember her saying to me, 'Relax, you'll like it.'" Alison head dropped to her hands. "She was grinding on me. I tried to push her off." She lifted her head. "She touched my breast again…the feeling excited me, but I didn't want to do anything."

Doctor Rios handed her the flowered kleenex box. "I'm sorry. What happened after that?" She sat down.

She wiped her eyes. "My friend Tim, he rescued me from that horrible woman."

"There are a few symptoms you have described, stress and mood swings. Those and a few more can be categorized under Bipolar one. Medication can help—"

"I don't want to take medication. I'm not crazy." She stood.

The doctor clasped her hands. "No, you're not crazy. Medication can help stabilize a chemical imbalance. But what I would like to do is approach this first with talk therapy."

"Talk therapy?"

"Psychotherapy known as talk therapy."

Alison giggled. "Okay." She smiled.

"Alison today was a good day. I want to meet with you again in a few weeks. Until then, what I want you to do is try to keep a journal and note any obvious change in your mood or if someone mentions it." The doctor scribbled in her notebook.

Alison gathered her belongings, pulled her cap down, and reached for the door. She turned to the doctor. "Thank you, Doctor Rios." She stretched her hand. "Should I bring Alan with me next time?"

"Let's discuss that at the next visit."

The women shook hands. Alison slowly strutted down the hall. Back at the empty waiting area, she made her next appointment.

CHAPTER 25

Alan

Alan yelled, "Daryl, turn that up. You know that's the jam." He dipped to "That's the Way I Like It" by KC and the Sunshine Band.

A couple of people stared regarding his and Daryl's indecent photo shot. He smiled and greeted his guests with warmth and hospitality no matter what. His teammates showed off their wild and funky colorful clothing. Alan sported a pair of blue jeans that hugged his bottom and thighs, yet flared like elephant ears at the ankles. His burgundy and white striped shirt complimented his broad shoulders and muscular arms. The leather white platform shoes with tassels hung over the sides looked like a two-layer coconut cake.

Everyone enjoyed themselves in the sunny and seventy-five-degree weather. Alison had catered from some of Atlanta's finest restaurants. Alan contributed with Alison in slicing the delicate kiwis, pineapples, strawberries, and mangos.

"Hey, baby." Alison wrapped her arms around Alan's waist.

Alan turned, bent down, and met his wife's soft lips. He rubbed her belly that peeked below a yellow strapless top. Alan's mouth desired her bare caramel shoulders. He gently kissed her on each and whispered, "Thank you for forgiving me, baby. I'm so sorry for that picture."

"Who said I forgave you for being so stupid to get caught up in mess?"

"Come on, baby, I know you can't still be mad…"

"Alan, I'm kidding, baby, of course I forgive you." Alison caressed his shoulder.

"Uh, oh, looks like we have a song to dance to."

He walked toward Daryl. "Bump that music man, this is a party and come over and join everyone."

Lipps Inc's "Funky Town" energized the crowd. Afros swayed in the movement of hysterical and retro dance moves. Alan looked to the west and saw a beautiful glow. The setting sun had nothing on this bronze statue. Tonya moved in slow motion as he became hypnotized. With each movement, her fiery red mini-skirt rose an inch more, exposing her thick legs. The white tube top hugged her firm breasts. Beneath the deep red lipstick, false lashes, and pearl eye shadow, Tonya's skin was flawless. The beauty mark on her left cheek freckles on her nose was sexually appealing.

"Enjoying yourself, Alan?" Tonya winked.

"Yeah, yeah, this is cool. Thank you for helping out." Alan took her arm and spun Tonya around.

"My pleasure and anytime you need my help let me know."

"You can help me get some more fruit from the house. I don't know where Alison disappeared too."

"Don't you guys have staff to help?" Tonya curved her lips.

"I thought we mentioned to you, since this is a small gathering, we gave the staff the day off. They are our guests. They deserve some down time and fun also." Alan led the way to the patio door.

"I knew there was something I loved about you, Alan Perry." Tonya brushed against his arm lightly.

Alan carried a serving dish of sliced fruit to the makeshift serving table while Tonya assisted with the dips and whipped cream. Alan watched her slowly lick the smooth sweet cream from a strawberry. He was beyond himself with fascination and fantasy. He better get a grip before things got out of control.

As night fell, Alan lit the back-yard tiki torches. He stood with Alison beside him when the karaoke began. Daryl and Tonya belted the lyrics to "Le Freak" by Chic. Everyone bopped their heads to the upbeat disco savvy.

"Alan, look at Daryl with those tight black polyester pants and that white ruffled shirt and collar touching each shoulder." Alison covered her mouth to hold the laugh.

"Don't be teasing my boy. This is a '70s party and in my opinion, missy, Daryl is the sharpest one here."

Once Daryl and Tonya finished their rendition of the song, Tonya gladly accepted a dry martini. Too many to count.

"Alison, excuse me for a minute. I think Tonya had too many drinks."

"She's enjoying herself."

"Yeah, but not at our expense that she goes out of here and have an accident. I'll be back."

"Hey, Tonya, come inside for a moment." As Alan led Tonya into the house, she stumbled into his arms.

"You want me don't you, Alan." Tonya lay her head on his chest.

The softness from her body tickled Alan's. He took her by the arm. "Tonya, you had too many drinks. I think it's time to stop." He took the glass away as she sipped.

"Alan." She stumbled forward. "I know when enough is enough. I'm not drunk, tipsy maybe, but not drunk. I like to have all my senses when things happen, you know what I mean?" She winked.

Alan removed a half-gallon pitcher of ice water from the fridge. "Start drinking this. It'll help dilute that alcohol."

"You're so sweet, Alan. How I wish I had a man like you or better can I just have you? I'm kidding, silly, but you are a good man and I hope to find someone like you." She kissed him on the cheek and slender fingers curved around a cold glass and she sipped the water.

People started to leave. Alan, Daryl, and a couple of the team cleaned the back yard. Alan had removed all the torches except one.

As he bent down to pick up party streamers a light touch trailed his shoulders. Alan stomach quivered.

"Baby, I'm exhausted. I'm turning in. Can you handle this?"

"Yeah, I got it you go ahead and get comfortable. I'll be in soon as I can. Did you see Tonya? I gave her a pitcher of water to drink." Alan laughed. "She claimed she wasn't drunk."

"I saw her a while ago talking to Daryl. I think she left."

Alan's brows met as he squinted. "Hmm, I hope she's okay."

"I'm sure she's fine."

***

"Daryl give me a hand with this table." The two hefty guys lifted the table with ease. They folded legs under and stacked the table on top of others. Alan fought the desires that had built from watching Tonya all night. She was beautiful, but tonight she was sexually appealing. His desire to have her heightened.

"She's still here man…" Daryl whispered.

"Who?"

Daryl pulled Alan by the collar. "You know who," he pointed to a dark corner of the yard. Tonya sat in a chaise lounge with the pitcher of water besides her. With legs crossed she smiled and waved at Alan.

Alan gave a slight wave, but a toothy smile. "I thought she was gone?"

"So, you're glad she's still here, huh?"

"I'm surprised."

Daryl wiped his hands on a flowered paper towel. "Okay, Alan, whatever you say. Look, are we done here because I have a late-night snack." Daryl rubbed his chin.

"Finished, help me carry these tables over there and you can go."

"Man, this party was great. Not too many people, just enough. I heard that picture, those women, received ten-grand for. We were suspended and fined over some bull shit for ten-grand?"

"Daryl, we shouldn't have been there mistake number one. Mistake number two, we shouldn't have been there, but what's done is done. We're lucky to get only a two-game suspension."

Alan finished cleaning and putting things back in order. He put out the last torch and walked to Tonya. She stood to meet him and they embraced. Alan kissed her.

"What's that for, Mr. Perry?"

Alan stared at the woman he fantasized about all night long. "I'm sorry, I shouldn't have done that Tonya."

Tonya gently placed his hand on her breast. She stood on her toes, grabbed his head, and guided him down toward her lips and kissed him deeply.

"Tonya, we can't do this." He wasn't sure of himself. Good, bad, and confusion trapped Alan.

Tonya pushed him down on the chaise and unsnapped his jeans. She placed her hand inside his underwear and squeezed him. "Are you sure, we can't?" She continued to squeeze him.

Alan breathed harder.

Tonya continued until she probed him out of his underwear. She licked her lips. His body jerked, tensed, and relaxed. Moments of intense play caused Alan to release his guilt.

"This will be our secret, Alan." Tonya took a swallow from the pitcher of water and left Alan to lay in darkness.

A single tear found its way from his eye.

CHAPTER 26

Drew

Drew sat back on the two-tone brown and burgundy tweed sofa. With feet propped on an ottoman, he sipped chardonnay. He occasionally looked at his cell phone. His attention went back to the double hung window and through it he watched mother nature spew her white dust across New York. The chill and wind formed some of the white dust into ice against the window. Another sip from the glass and he reached for the cell phone.

"Hello," a hoarse Alison answered.

Drew smiled. "Hey, sweetie, how are you?"

Alison yawned. "Drew, hey, what time is it?"

"Eleven p.m. I was thinking about you. Is it too late, is Alan there?"

"You're funny. I know you follow the game and Alan is away. But yes, it would be too late if he was here. Are you okay?"

Drew's heart was heavy with confusion, regret, and resentment. His only regret was letting Alison go. He should've fought for her, but time moved on and she is deeply in love with Alan. Alan had always been a pain in Drew's back end. Then and now they were rivals except now they'd added a tad bit of maturity to it. Drew respected Alan, though he didn't believe they would ever sit down and chit-chat like old friends. Alan was a prissy jock who used his good looks to get women. Drew was down and dirty and to the point. He gave women what they wanted—a good stiffness and sometime a little roughness for the added flare, but he never abused them. The bad boy, most women called him.

"Alison, I called because I want Janice back, but she's making this difficult for me. I gave in the other night with my soon-to-be baby momma."

"Come on, Drew, what's the matter with you? The last time we talked you were going to work on this…"

Drew huffed. He slowly poured another glass of chardonnay and stood by the window. "Don't lecture me, Alison." Drew kept his tone leveled. What can I do if Janice won't try? I think she believe this shit is funny. I don't find it to be funny the least bit."

"Drew, listen to me. I may be the wrong person to give advice, right now you need to hear me. Janice, I'm quite sure, doesn't think this is funny, but she is hurting. Tell me this, how in the hell do you think she's supposed to feel, you screwed another woman and have a baby on the way?"

"Damn girl." He laughed.

"Grow up, Drew. You called me with the problem that you created. If you don't want to hear the truth then we can talk about something else."

Quietness swept across the line so that he could hear Mother Nature's breath beat against the windows.

"Alison, that's what I love about you. You're honest."

"Hmph."

"What was that for?"

"I'm learning to be more honest with myself, but anyway go ahead."

He turned from the window and stared at the clock, which now read midnight. In the dimly lit kitchen Drew placed the empty wine glass in the stainless-steel sink, which he leaned against and crossed his legs. "I promise you this, and I will be a better man because this isn't the way I want to live. I love my wife and I'll do whatever its going to take to make our relationship work."

"What about the resentment you feel towards Janice for breaking us up?"

"We need to seek counseling for a lot of things. I have to forgive her. You forgave me." Drew wiped his eyes carefully and dared not to let a tremble enter his voice. "Alison, thank you. I promise you I'm going to change, believe me. At this point in my life I don't' feel as though I have many truthful friends. You and Tim have been very supportive and with every breath I take, I'm going to fight to be a better man. I'll call you in the New Year with good news, you wait and see.

CHAPTER 27

Drew

"I'm happy you asked me to come over, Drew. I know things have been hectic at work…"

"With your persistent behavior, Mallory, I'm surprised we're not fired." Drew offered her a seat.

"It's hard to be around you and not have you, especially after that last get together. I'm so sorry for all the things I've done…"

"Does that include going to my home?" Drew eyebrows raised.

Mallory squinted and her chest rose. She meant everything that had happened, whether she admitted it or not.

"Like I said, I'm sorry for things I've done. Why did you ask me to come over? Mallory helped herself to a handful of cashews that sat in a miniature crystal serving bowl.

We need to talk about this entire situation thoroughly and thoughtful."

"Drew." She licked her fingers, "I agree because the first thing is what type of visitation do you want? I'm more than willing to grant you joint custody—"

"That's what I'm talking about…"

"As I was saying," Mallory swallowed more water, "joint custody…only and I mean o-n-l-y, if Janice isn't around our baby."

How in the hell did she think *that* was going to work? Not that Drew expected her to think, but he had to know.

"Mallory, I told you I want my marriage to work with Janice and she was the one hurt in this. Why are you being this way?" I thought you understood when we last talked?"

"I thought you were getting back with me when you came over and fucked me."

Anger built around the muscles in his stomach. He didn't know what to do nor say.

"Look, Drew, I don't want some mad, black, ghetto—"

"Watch your mouth or I'll beat that kid right out of you."

"I understand you're angry," Mallory moved from the sofa, "but with Janice all I'm saying is I don't know her and she may hurt our baby."

"I know Janice and she won't do anything like that."

"My point is I don't know her and if you want joint custody with no complications for visitation then that's my offer."

"You can't do this."

"Watch me. I suggest you think long and hard about what's more important to you—your baby that you can have around for life or a woman that will up and leave you with the change of seasons."

Mallory stood and nibbled on more of the salty cashews with a smirk.

By the grace of God, he Didn't knock it off.

CHAPTER 28

Alan

The late hours had consumed Alan. Days ago, he flew home from a game in Minnesota, which was a victory dance for Alan and his teammates. Upon arriving home that night Alison stood in the foyer. He smelt the fresh fragrance of bloomed flowers. Without exchanging any words, he took his wife hand and led her up the stairs. Alan took a shower and rested in bed with Alison.

Three days had passed since he romantically gave his wife attention yet his mind was obsessed with another thought. He lay on the deep plush sofa with lights dimmed and listened to the smooth svelte sounds of Damien Escobar, the violinist. Alan massaged himself. His mind consumed more of the enticing night he had with Tonya. He massaged more. The music continued. Alan couldn't control the urge that grew within him. He had to have her. Was it just an animal attraction, was it just being a man to conquer, or was he bored with his wife? He lay his back onto the sofa and let his mind drift into the feeling. Alan had nearly reached his climax when something vibrated. "Ah, no." He tried to continue, but the annoying vibration of his cellphone continued.

He swiped to answer. "What!"

"Did I catch you at a bad time?" Tonya's voice was sultry and inviting.

Alan almost went limp from the distraction, but her voice brought back the excitement he needed. He calmed himself enough to answer, "No, not at all…" He bit his bottom lip and continued, "I was thinking about you." He steadied his breathing.

"Really now, what's on your mind?"

"To be honest, Tonya, I don't know. There's something about you and I know it's wrong for me to have the thoughts that I do, but I can't explain it."

"You want me, Alan, you can have me. I told you that it could be our little secret."

"How can you say you are friends with my wife and want to get with me?"

Tonya replied, "How can you say you love your wife and want to get with me?"

"I love my wife regardless, but I don't want you throwing this up in her face. Shit, I'm no better than you."

"We haven't done anything. I have done you of course so why you're feeling so guilty. Is there something you're not telling me?"

"I already told you that it's something about you and that added little thing you did after the party intensified what I was feeling."

"Did it now? Let's stop playing games. Do you want to hook-up?"

This was a good time to get it out his system. "Yeah, let's. Is tomorrow night cool? Alison's mom is visiting. They can have time to catch up."

"Then it's a date. You come over and I'll cook."

"Oh, we doing all that? Eating…"

"I treat my men right."

"Where will Asia be?"

"At my neighbors."

"Again?" Alan adjusted himself upward.

"They're like family very supportive since Eric left."

"Do you still talk to him?"

"Not really, since he's married. I can't stomach that uppity bitch."

The words that smoothly slipped from Tonya's mouth took Alan by surprise. He had never heard her say one bad thing about anyone, except her baby's father.

"So, you want me to come over there. Sounds good."

"Don't you think we'll have more of a good time in private?"

"We'll see. I'll call you tomorrow."

The aroma of sizzling bacon, hot buttered grits, biscuits, and rich hazelnut coffee woke Alan who slept in his shorts and t-shirt. He staggered out of the family room only to find his mother-in-law staring in his face.

"Alan, why are you sleeping in that room and not with your wife?

Too early in the morning for Alan to be questioned, especially in his home by a guest. I dozed off. When did you get here?" Alan took his forefinger to get sleep from his eyes.

"About an hour ago, your wife, my daughter came to get me from the airport, while you slept all morning."

All morning. 8 a.m. stared him in the face through his watch. His mother-in-law was a good woman, but too much attitude. Sometime he wondered who wore the pants in her family.

"Moms, there's nothing wrong with Alison coming to get you. Alison didn't want to wake me I'm sure and it wasn't a difficult task to drive to the airport. If it was too hard for her, she would've awakened me or called a car for you." Alan turned to walk away.

"How's your girlfriend doing?"

"Excuse me? What did you say—"

"Hey baby, good morning." Alison hugged him tightly around the waist. "I see you and Momma are talking."

"Yeah, your mother wanted to know why I didn't come with you to pick her up." Alan sneered toward his mother-in-law.

Alan rushed up the stairs and into the master bathroom. A few minutes later Alison quietly stepped in while he showered.

"Alan, what's going on with you and Mom?"

"You know what, I'm not going there with your mother. As long as she's in my house she needs to respect me. I don't have time for her assumptions and interrogation."

"Wow, what did she say to you?"

"It doesn't matter, that's your mother, and you spend some time with her. Later I'm going out with Daryl and it might be a long night."

"Come on, my mother just got here and you're abandoning me?"

"I'm not abandoning you. That's your mother and you should spend time with her. Besides, right now I'm not in the mood to be around her."

"What about breakfast? I cooked your favorite."

Alan stepped from the shower and Alison head was hung low, lips turned down, and arms crossed. From a stack of folded towels, Alan wrapped his waist tightly. He wiped the steam from mirror, flexed, and admired his muscular build. When he turned to Alison, she now bore a tight lip and squinted eyes.

"Why are you angry at me? Your mother is the one that started this, Alison."

"Why are you blaming my mother? What do you think she's going to say when you walk out of here and be gone all night?"

The sport scent deodorant glided with each stroke Alan gave.

"Did you hear what I said? What is my mother going—"

"Alison, listen, I really don't care what your mother is going to say. She's not my mother and better yet I'm a grown man and I do what I damn well please."

Kissing Mrs. Jackson behind wasn't on Alan's agenda, especially after accusing him having a girlfriend.

"Alison, I'll be down soon. But I'm still going out later and your mother has nothing to do with this. I don't want her causing problems for us, baby."

Alan knew this fight was more of his ego and what dangled between his legs. He reached for Alison and looked at her.

"I'm being an ass and I'm sorry. Hey, do you want me to go with you on your next appointment?"

"You know Alan, I think I'm good. I can handle this on my own."

He bent down to kiss her forehead, but she walked away.

***

"So, your mother-in-law accused you of having a girlfriend?"

"She did." Alan forked a piece of the baked trout.

With her head leaning to one side, Tonya asked, "What is going on with us, Alan?"

"Ha." With food still in his mouth Alan was inaudible. "This food is what's going on. It's delicious."

Tonya moved closer to Alan and leaned into his ear. "If you think the food is good then you should try me." She licked his ear.

Alan placed his fork on the plate. He kissed her deeply. He pushed the dishes away and lay Tonya on her back. He stood and admired her beauty. He remembered the night at the club when she seduced him with a dance. He remembered the episode in his back yard. He watched her squirm on the table with simple, but yet seductive moves. Alan picked her up and walked to the bedroom. Red and white candles greeted them with a hint of vanilla and spice. While he kissed her neck, Alan lay her on the bed.

Tonya stroked Alan's thick arms and moved to his face. She gently rubbed each side then held tightly as she forced her mouth to his. Alan removed her blouse, bra, and pants. He pulled back to look at her perky round breasts and the beautiful red-laced underwear that graced her bottom. He slid the underwear off and licked Tonya's legs. All of Alan's thoughts became reality. Her body was so very soft. Tonya lifted and re-positioned herself underneath him, allowing Alan to press against her hot spot.

"Alan, you don't have to be afraid of me. I won't say a word. Remember, this is our secret. No one will ever know." She kissed him.

"Are you sure because I don't need any trouble." He gyrated on her. "I'm not afraid of you by the way."

"Then show me what you have in those pants."

Alan jumped to his feet, unzipped the jeans and pulled them down with the underwear in one motion.

Tonya's eyes bulged.

Alan reached inside the jean pocket and fumbled. He found what he looked for in a blue packet.

Tonya took it. "Alan, we don't need this. I'm on the pill and I want to feel you, the bare you."

With no hesitation Alan stimulated Tonya's hot spot with his finger. He kept going until she joined in self-pleasure. Alan watched for a moment while he did the same to himself. The night before in his family room was interrupted, but tonight he thought, would certainly be finished.

Soft moans escaped from Tonya. Time to see what all the hoopla was about. "Tonya, come here, baby." He moved her hands and held them above her head. He lowered his body until his mouth touched her. He gently licked her a few times then went faster. She jerked and tried to free her hands, but he held tightly. He repeated the motion until her body released the juices he longed for. He released her hands and positioned his body on top of hers. Ever so slowly, he inched his massive erection into her wetness. Tonya moved at a jack rabbit speed. Determined to keep up and not out done, Alan went faster. Her strong legs wrapped tightly around his back as she held on.

Alan sat back and placed her legs on his shoulders. Her short mane was matted to her head. His body glistened in the candle light.

"Alan, I want to go for a ride," Tonya nearly out of breath whispered.

With the change of position, Alan and Tonya rocked the satin sheets until midnight.

CHAPTER 29

Drew

New York had better days with winter, but as Drew sat at his desk and stared out the window the snow continued to fall. Ten inches sprawled out overnight. He left for work two hours earlier to make it in on time. He turned his attention back to the stack of unopened interoffice envelopes and dreaded the outcome. Lately, he seemed to have more work than he could handle.

"Excuse me." A light knock at the opened door startled him. "There's a Mr. Jackson here to see you."

"Yeah, yeah, let him in and any time he comes, Leah, it's okay."

"Yes, sir." The slim Gal Gadot look alike stepped aside for the visitor to enter.

"Damn man, who is that?" Tim's voiced was hushed.

"Leah, my new secretary."

"You got rid of that crazy girl?"

Drew was tired of the name calling, threats, and secrets. "Mallory decided to apply for the administrative position down on four. She's trying to show me that she's not the evil person I think."

"Is it working?" Tim sat in the leather chair.

"There's nothing she can do that'll change my mind except if she stop black mailing me with my own baby." Drew fumbled through the stacks of envelopes.

Tim coughed. "She's what? Now what the hell is she doing?"

Drew stood and closed the door. He filled Tim in on everything that transpired the day he slept with Mallory, again to her last visit.

"Your fist mistake was hopping in bed with her again. What were you *thinking*?" Tim stated.

"Please, Tim, don't start your bullshit again. I do not need a lecture. I know what I did, it was wrong, and I told Mallory that. I don't want her. I want to have a co-parent relationship and not under her crazy terms."

Drew tapped on the desk. Taking the picture from his desk he stood. "You see this woman?" He pointed to the picture. "I love Janice. I made a mistake and through hell or high water, I'm going to make this right."

He leaned on the window. Slow and steady breaths formed a mist. Drew raised his right arm and leaned his forehead on it. While He rested, his cell phone vibrated. Private appeared on the display. Drew answered. Silence.

"Drew, I get it. I wasn't lecturing you. You know man, I see a big improvement with you. The fact you weren't all over that new secretary of yours is a plus." They laughed.

"Alison told me to get my shit together if—"

"When did you talk to her?"

"Dude what's your problem, you the one that can call her at home anytime you want and hell she came to stay with you."

"I haven't spoken to her since I told her about my situation."

Drew's eyes widened. "You told her. How did she take it?" He leaned on the desk.

"She was all right with it, kind of hurt that I didn't tell he the truth sooner."

"That's Alison, she's a very understanding person and have a good heart. I hope that husband of hers doesn't hurt her. You know he already done that with those pictures."

"I know. But she's a strong woman, she'll be fine. Now what are you going to do?"

"I'm going to get my wife back."

Tim left and Drew picked up the envelopes. One by one he opened them and to his surprise a note scribbled in red ink fell out.

"Drew you are on my mind every day and night, so much that I can't sleep. Why don't you see that we belong together? I try to think what the hell went wrong so that I can fix it. I think you're going to break my heart, but please consider that if you leave, I'll lose a part of me. I never loved as I love you."

Drew tossed the note into the paper shredder and laughed. She was not going to get him this time with her delirious sayings.

His desk phone buzzed. Drew nearly jumped from his seat. "I'm sorry to disturb you, but your wife is on line one."

In a hurry, Drew reached for the phone." Thanks, Leah. Hey, baby, how are you? Hello…hello." He quickly dialed Janice's number.

"Janice, why did you hang up?"

"What are you talking about?"

"When I answered you hung up…"

"I guess your crazy-ass girlfriend is playing games because I didn't call you."

He was relieved that Janice hadn't hung up, yet upset that Mallory was behind the confusion.

"Janice, she's not my girlfriend and I'm sorry for thinking that you would do that. Since I have you on the phone can we talk?"

In a low voice Janice answered, "It's time we do."

Signs of good things were to come as Drew and Janice relived their past, dealt with the present, and prepared for the future.

CHAPTER 30

Alison

One thing Alison loved about living in Atlanta was little to no snow and moderate weather during the winter months. Just like when she was a kid in Mississippi, all year-round beautiful weather.

The winds were brisk. "Gusty winds, but mild temperatures in the low to mid-fifties will give Atlanta the coldest so far for the year," the broadcaster, on the weather channel, said.

Alison held a cup of herbal tea and watched the leaves dance gracefully around the yard. She was startled by the chimes of the doorbell. Checking the video camera, she saw Tonya's car and pushed the entry button. Alison sat the tea cup down, brushed back her hair, and smoothed her slinky red gaucho romper. The halter neckline outfit hugged Alison's body. Beyoncé had nothing on this. As she walked to the door, the red crocodile open toe sling backs added more length to Alison's legs.

"Tonya, what a surprise."

"I hope this isn't a bad time. You want to have lunch today?"

"Oh, no, I can't my mom is visiting."

"I completely forgot. Alan told me that."

"Well, come, you can meet her."

Alison led the way to the kitchen when she spotted Alan darting to the family room.

"Hi, Alan," Tonya blurted, causing Alison's mom to frown.

"Hey, Tonya, what's up?" Alan said slowly.

Asia ran into Alan's arms while Alison stopped in front of her mom.

Alison extended her hand toward Tonya. "Momma, I want you to meet—"

"So, this is the girl?"

"Momma, don't start okay," Alison whispered.

"I can't start something if there isn't anything to start." She huffed at Tonya.

Tonya reached for her hand. "Mrs. Jackson, I've heard wonderful things about you."

"Did you now, quite tell what would that have been?"

"Alison has mentioned how supportive you are and—"

"Did she also mention how protective I am? She tilted her designer glasses.

"I gathered that, Mrs. Jackson. I am a mother also and wouldn't let anyone hurt my child." Tonya uneasily smiled.

Thicker than pea soup, the tension had grown in the room.

"Alison is this the girl?" Her mother peered over the glasses.

"Momma." Alison lowered her voice.

"Am I the girl? What's going on?" Tonya looked around the room.

"Well, my daughter told me there was some girl hanging around her husband a lot and she didn't feel comfortable with that?" Alison tried to pull her mother to the side. "So, I guess it's you."

It had become awkward for the four of them. Alison looked at her mother and gasped. Then she caught the sights of Alan. But it was Tonya's stare that burned into Alison.

"Alison what did you tell your mother about me?" Tonya stood tall.

Everyone looked at Alison. She felt low.

"Alison, baby, tell the truth. You don't like Alan spending time with that girl. It's okay."

"No, momma. You were wrong. That was between us and I could handle Alan."

"Handle me. Wait." Alan's arms were up as to signal a field goal. "There's nothing to handle here. Why are you talking to your mom about me...handling me—"

"That's not how the conversation went Alan. Besides, I have told you I didn't know why she always wanted to be around you—"

"Her wanting to be around me is not saying you had a problem with me." Alan shook his head.

Tonya took Asia by the hand. "Alison, I thought we were friends. I sat here and cried to you about my problems—"

"Everybody, shut up!" Alison pointed to each one. "Tonya you need to leave. Momma, I need some time with my husband."

Her mother adjusted the eyeglasses. "I told you the truth before and that girl wants your husband and she's going to get him if you don't wise up. It irks me that you choose not to know this. Baby, if you don't open your eyes and wise up, that little hussy is going to sashay herself right into your bed, your house and your family."

With her back to her mom, Alison asked her mother in a simple yet sad tone to leave.

***

Eyes filled with tears Alison looked at Alan. She didn't want to, but she had to talk to him. "Alan." She placed her hand on his chest. "I know you're angry, but I swear I was not talking behind your back."

"If you had a problem with Tonya coming over here...why were you hanging out with her? Why did you want to have that party, with her, assisting?" He pushed her hand off his chest.

"Okay, I had a problem with her hanging around you all the time, but you surely didn't seem to mind. I shouldn't have to tell you; you know when and if a woman is getting too friendly. You should've said something."

"Hold up…stop right there, "Alan's voice deepened, "you're not going to blame this on me when your mother blabbed what you told her. She's the one who put you on blast." He wiped his mouth. "Your mother has no respect for us or our home."

"You don't respect my mother or me." Calmly, Alison spoke. "Maybe you need to leave and clear your mind."

Alan's head turned once then again, eyes squinted, and brows bunched. "I don't believe this you putting me out my house? This is some crazy bullshit."

"Alan please! Alison fanned her hand.

"I don't know what's gotten into you, but I seriously hope you figure it out before it's too late. Matter of fact when is your next doctor appointment?"

"What do you mean too late. And why do you need to know about my appointments. I've told you I can handle this."

"I'm tired of this, your up and down attitude." He went up the staircase and stopped at the landing, shrugged his shoulders and walked away.

CHAPTER 31

Alison

Weeks had passed and Alison was learning how to become a better her. She journaled every day and practice on reflection. Her mother was back home and called Alison every day reminding her of the big blow up. Alison, feeling more empowered and understanding her worth, peace, and happiness, she asked her mother not to call her every day and definitely not to bring up negative things.

"Alison, this is our fifth meeting now. How are you?"

"Doctor Rios, for the most part I'm okay. The talk therapy is working. I look back at my journal notes and a lot of my irritation comes from *me*. I need to speak up more and defend *me*. I have been trying to please and make everyone else happy. I internalized my anger.

"I see." The doctor smiled. "When you say everyone…"

"Yes." I have two friends, one being an ex-boyfriend, dumping his guilt and womanizing ways on me. He didn't say it was my fault, but because he didn't have me, but overall, he made decisions that caused a separation from his wife, baby, and baby momma drama. So, he calls me asking for forgiveness and advice." Alison sighed. "Then my friend that saved me from the rape…he has HIV." She clasped her hands together. Doctor Rios, I'm mentally drained. My husband and mother got into an argument over a female friend…well she's not my friend anymore and I've asked my husband to stop seeing her as well."

"It seems that you're the glue to three important people, but you are correct. Your happiness comes first."

Alison sat forward. "Doctor." She exhaled. "I want to have a baby with my husband. I was being selfish, especially these last few months. My selfishness, I think rubbed off on Alan."

Alison watched as Doctor Rios, nodded and jotted down notes.

"In what way do you think your selfishness rubbed off on Alan?"

"He loves me, I know. But he's short tempered with me. I would be with myself as well. Alan is really a sweet loving guy." Alison smiled. "When I think about the early days of us together, it was fun, exciting, spur of the moments, and quality time. I love having those moments, but I see my selfishness is getting in the way of our happiness. He has asked me many times about starting a family, but I kept avoiding it."

"And now you're ready for a change."

Her eyes gleamed. "I am!" Alison stood. "I am, Doctor Rios. I know my husband and I can always have those happy moments…and with a baby. Life is too short and I don't want my marriage to suffer."

Doctor Rios laid her pen down, adjusted her glasses, and smiled. "Alison, over these last weeks, you have made progress…and without medication. I don't believe at this time you need to go on with a Psychiatrist for medication. You and I can continue our sessions. I believe continuing with the journal and reflections, you will be better. We will continue the sessions on a monthly basis. Are you okay with that?"

Alison smoothed strands of her hair behind her ear. "Yes. Yes, I am."

CHAPTER 32

Drew

"Tim this is the happiest day of my life. Janice is on her way over to help me pack. I'm moving back home, man." Drew threw his hands to the heavens.

"Are you sure it's going to work out…you're ready to be faithful to your wife, dog?"

"Uh huh, I'm ready. Life is too short. Later I have to call Alison and tell her the good news. I promised her a call, promised her that I was going to get better."

"I'm happy for you and Janice. What made her take your silly ass back?"

"We had a long talk and she said it was better to forgive and move forward than holding resentment. What I really think changed her mind was the magic stick I gave her after dinner one night. Woof, woof," Drew barked.

"I'm sure that was it. She just let you back home like that?"

Drew laughed. "One of the requirements, I have to seek counseling about my *ways*. You know trying to get in bed with a lot of women. She doesn't want to accept that I made peace with Alison and I'm done. I'm cured."

"Cool. You better make it work this time."

"I got this; everything is going to be fine." Drew's second line beeped. "Hold on Tim. Hello, okay come on up. Tim, that's my baby. We're going to get packing so I can get the hell out of here. I can't wait to lay back in my bed, caressing my wife."

"All right, later dude, and don't forget to call Alison, I'm quite sure she'll be happy to hear from you."

***

Drew danced around the nearly empty apartment. He swooped down and back up, grabbed a pillow from the sofa, and pretended it was Janice's head against his chest. He spun around and hugged the pillow tightly. Lightly he placed his lips on it, giving his lady love a delicate kiss.

He was distracted with a light knock at the door. As he placed the pillow down, he lowered the stereo volume. He opened the door and smiled. His heart beat faster. This was a new feeling, something he never felt before, something real.

Janice stood at the door dressed in a black Nike velvet suit and black gym shoes. Underneath the jacket she sported a white mid-riff top. Drew admire the washboard stomach.

"Come on in, Janice." Drew struggled to maintain his urge to freak her right then. "Is that a belly ring?"

"You like it." She leaned back.

"I love it. Do you have any more somewhere maybe I can find?"

Janice rolled her tongue around her lips. "Not yet."

"You must be trying to make me hot up in here coming over in that body-hugging outfit. Don't you know how cold it is out there?"

Janice laughed. "Cold is an understatement. I nearly froze my butt off trying to look good for you. I left my coat in the car."

Drew pulled her close. "Baby, I don't need you to impress me to the point you may get sick or something. I love you for you. I am sorry that I let my selfishness get the best of me. I promise, baby, I am going to be the man that God have in store for me to be." Drew squinted back tears. "It means a lot that you forgave me, to give my stupid ass another chance, but I'm so thankful. I love you Janice." He kissed her fully.

"You've already apologized more ways than. Let's get this stuff out of here and back to the home where it belongs." Janice pecked him lightly on the cheek.

Hours had passed with laughter, deep s tares, and a light snack. Drew and Janice carried boxes to their cars. As Janice walked up the steps, Drew there a fist-size snowball at her back. He picked up more snow and rolled it between his hands. Janice ran toward him and slipped.

"Are you all right?" Drew knelt to help his wife stand up.

"I'm fine," Janice grabbed a handful of snow, "Sucker." She covered Drew's face. And trotted up the stairs.

"Wait till I get you." Drew chased behind.

Janice said, "Drew, I'm sorry also. I love you, baby, and I'm glad we're having another chance at love. This time we're going to make it right."

"We will make it better. Drew hugged her. "I'm going to be the best husband. You deserve it."

A knock at the door. "Who could be knocking on this door. Who in the hell?" Drew pulled away from Janice.

"Don't answer it maybe they'll go away."

"It'll be quick. Let me see who it is." Drew strutted to the door. Looking over his shoulder he winked and sent a floating kiss.

Once the door opened all smiles dropped. Janice's hands rested on her hips, Drew's eyes bulged, and the visitor blankly stared.

"What are you doing here?"

"I didn't know you had company, but I came to see if you thought about what we discussed, you know about the arrangement for the baby?"

"Mallory, this isn't the right time—"

Janice said, "This is a good time, Drew. We all can get to the heart of the matter. "

Mallory's head flipped around. "Excuse me, you don't have anything to do with this. This is between Drew and I and only us. Why are you here anyway?"

"For your information this has everything to do with me since my husband is coming back home with me. You will hear from our attorney regarding visitation and so forth."

"Drew, are you going to let this woman speak to me this way. I'm carrying your baby for God's sake."

"Mallory, that's my wife and she has every right to be included in this. I already told you that nothing is happening between you and I. As my wife said, you will hear from our attorney. I won't be black mailed into being with you or seeing my child."

"If you don't mind, Mallory." Janice smirked. "You need to leave so that we can get back to doing what we were doing"

With her hand in the black winter coat, Mallory stepped closer to Janice. Out came a Pro Trophy Skinner knife. Blood gushed from Janice's face. Mallory had sliced upward then across her face, missing Janice's right eye by centimeters.

Drew dashed to Mallory. She turned with the knife pointed outward and Drew landed on it. Wounded in the side, Drew managed to stand slightly and continued his efforts. "You crazy bitch, you're going to die for this."

Mallory smiled. "I won't be too sure of that."

As Drew stumbled toward her, Mallory grabbed Drew around the neck and cut. Drew grabbed his neck, staggered backward, fell to the floor, and shook uncontrollably. Mallory knelt over him and continued to stab Drew continually until life in his eyes went dark.

Janice had managed to dial 911. She dropped the phone, call still connected, and crawled to Drew.

Mallory stood over Drew's bloody body and wickedly laughed. "You black bitch. If I couldn't have him neither could you. Oh, and this baby won't breathe a day of fresh air." Mallory stabbed herself in the stomach and pulled the knife upward.

Janice screamed as Mallory's body fell limp next to Drew's. Janice scooted next to Drew's other side and grabbed his hand. She whispered lightly into his ear, "Wake up, Drew. Please, baby, wake up. You promised that you would be a better husband for me." Tears mixed with blood ran down Janice's face as she lay her head on her husband's beatless chest.

CHAPTER 33

Tim

"I'm sorry, Alison. "Tim sniffed, "Drew is gone. He got caught up with that girl."

"This can't be real…"

"Wait, it's on the news let me turn the volume up so you can hear."

"This is Dari Alexander for Fox 5 New York's news at 6, we have breaking news. Last night Drew Langston was tragically murdered. His wife, Janice Langston, was injured, but survived. The attacker, Mallory James, apparently took her life as well as unborn child.

"Alison, do you hear it?"

"Yes, that's enough I don't want to hear anymore." Alison sniffled.

"Did he call you?"

"No…" She sniffed again. "He was going to call and keep me updated on his new transformation." She gave a weak snicker."

"We talked last night and I told him to make sure he didn't forget, but I guess—"

"Why did this have to happen, Tim, why? He didn't deserve this."

"The only thing we can say is, it was his time. I feel sorry for Janice though.'

"How is she holding up? I know this just happened, but, Tim, she's going to need all the support there is now and after…"

In a low voice Tim said, "The funeral, are you coming?"

"I don't want to intrude. You know how Janice felt about me, but I will send flowers."

"I understand. How's things been going with you?"

Alison took a deep breath. "I have been seeing a therapist, you know for my mood swings—"

"A therapist. Is it that serious?"

"I'm okay. A therapist isn't bad. Someone to help me figure out how to manage my anger or stress. Hey, Tim, if at any point, I was flip floppy with you, I apologized for that. I have something I'm going to talk to Alan about as well. You know trying to keep my marriage intact."

"What do you have in mind to tell him?"

"I'll let you know after I do."

"Baby girl, everything will be all right just believe and talk with Alan."

"Tim, I love you too."

"What. I didn't say anything."

"You did months ago when you told me about your illness, remember?"

Tim flicked through the channels. "Good memory, baby girl. You'll always be a part of my heart and life Alison, always."

"I know and tell Janice I'm truly sorry for her loss."

CHAPTER 34

Alan

"Alan, thanks for being the gentleman that you are. When I was over there last, I don't know why Alison's mom attacked me like that?"

"Don't worry about it. I consider it old news. Just don't let it get you down."

"Where's the wife?"

"She wanted to be alone for a while. She just got word that an ex-boyfriend of hers was stabbed to death by his mistress."

"Get out, are you serious?"

"Very much, I mean from what she told me the girl that did this was crazy as a bat."

"What happened to the girl?"

Alan let the vanilla coke glide down his throat. "Dead." He exhaled, "she killed herself and the unborn baby."

Quiet, crept from Tonya's end back to Alan. Tonya cleared her throat. "Oh, she was pregnant."

"I don't know what I would do if someone killed my baby." Alan munched on chips.

"Alan, if it's possible I need you to come over just for a little while."

"I don't know, Tonya, this is sort of a bad time with the news Alison received and—"

"Please…I never begged you before, for anything, but this one thing I need you here, please."

"If it's that important I'll see what I can do."

"Thanks Alan."

What was a man to do? Torn between two women? He owed it to Alison to be by her side and for that matter Tonya's too, since he swayed between the sheets with her on more than one occasion now. Little thought he gave, but Tonya had become his mistress as well. He found himself paying her utilities and essentials. He even tossed a couple of hundred on a new wardrobe.

He tiptoed through the open kitchen and stopped. He looked at the copper pots that hung above the counter where he and Alison enjoyed a romantic interlude. He did not know what he was doing, but common sense had left long ago. Slowly, he walked to the foyer. With his head hung down, he trudged up the staircase.

At the landing he looked at the different portraits. He in his football uniform, kneeling, holding the ball in a throwing position. A picture of him standing tall, with jeans, cowboy boots, black tee shirt, fitted black cap, and hands behind his back. To his right, a picture of Alison. She looked so soft and elegant. He admired her long frame draped in an ivory layered gown. Diamonds and pearls dressed her arms. Another picture, Alison's smile was wide. She looked happy to him. She leaned to smell a bouquet of flowers. Her fitted jeans, accented her bottom. Her waist peeked beneath a pale pink belly top.

He didn't know how he got to the state of mind he was in and now would be the best time to end the carefree affair he allowed to settle into his marriage.

"Hey, Alison, how you doing?" Alan lay next to her.

"I'm okay. I feel sorry for Janice though; she has been through a lot with Drew. They were going to work out the situation and his life was snuffed out—" Alison sobbed into her hands as Alan rubbed her shoulders.

"It'll be all right, I promise. "Hey, I'm going to run out…to the store. Do you want something, ice-cream maybe?"

"Alan, I want a baby."

Alan looked around the room. "What did you say?" He sat completely up.

"I want to have a baby…with you. I realized how important it is for us. I am so sorry for being selfish. I don't want to lose what you and I have and now hearing what happened to Drew, life is too short."

"Thank you, Alison." He embraced her. "You continue to rest; I'll be back with the ice cream. We can continue this conversation okay, baby." He kissed her. He loved her.

Alan knew what he had to do. End the affair.

***

Alan sped on I270 and listened to Toni Braxton's *Secrets* cd. In front of Tonya's home, he sat for a moment. He loved his wife too much to allow his behavior to continue. If Alison found out, she would definitely file for divorce. And now she tells him she wants a baby. This was all he wanted…to complete his family, a baby. Alan sat there in the car. He contemplated how he would tell Tonya. Maybe assure her, she was a great person, but this thing they had, had to stop. Or maybe, he thought. He could look her in the eyes and say it's over and leave. Whatever he decided, it needed to be done. He pulled the hoodie up and stepped from the car. Briskly, he walked towards the dark home. Before he could ring the bell, Tonya appeared in the doorway.

"I thought you were going to sit out there all night." She pulled him in.

"No just, um, thinking."

Tonya frowned. "Thinking about what?"

Alan paced the floor. "Tonya, I like you a lot, but my family means so much to me. I don't know how you and I got to this point, but—"

"What do you mean your family?"

He turned to her. Palms up. "Alison told me she wants to have a baby."

Tonya, wringing her hands, "Alan, I'm pregnant?"

"Say what?" Alan head snapped.

Tonya reached for Alan. He pulled back.

"Alan, please, I found out today…"

"What do you mean you found out today…can't you women tell sooner?"

"I'm a month late and I decided to take a test today and—"

"And I thought you were on the pill. What happened with that?"

Tonya tried to hold Alan. "I sort of forgot some days."

"You forget to buy milk or you forget to renew a membership, but you don't fucking forget to take your birth control pills, Tonya." He rubbed his chin and turned quickly. "You forgetting to take your pills and Alison sneaking behind my back taking hers. What the fuck?"

Tonya wiped her eyes. "Alan, I forgot. I'm sorry."

"What are you going to do?" Alan stood erect.

"If you're insinuating that I have an abortion, you're crazy. That's why I called you over so we can discuss this."

"Forgive me for saying, but I'm not leaving my wife."

"I figured you would say that; you're a good man and I wouldn't have expected less."

"So, what is your plan? You're going to tell Alison that some stranger fathered your baby?" Alan breathed heavily.

"We're not going to tell her anything. I told you before this love affair is our secret. She never has to know."

Alan rubbed his head. "How do you plan for this to work, besides if her mother finds out—"

"There's nothing here for me in Atlanta anymore except you and I can't have you. Tonya slowly exhaled. I've decided to relocate. Of course, with your help?"

"I knew it." Alan shook his head in disbelief. "That's the catch huh?"

"Damn it, Alan, there's no fucking catch. I can't possibly afford to pick up and leave town, you of all people know that. If you pay for a down payment on a place to live, give me some money for a few months of expenses, I should be fine. I was online earlier today searching for jobs in Chicago."

"That's all you want? What about the baby?"

"That's your decision solely. If you want to help me out then we can work that out or if you want nothing to do with this child that's fine also, but I hope you try to have some interest in your baby's life."

Alan sat on the sofa with his head in his hands. He looked up at Tonya and pulled her close until his face was against her stomach. "I can't let you raise this baby without any support from me. I'll help you, but Alison can't find out about this baby, fuck, at least not now."

Tonya wrapped her arms around his head. "I know, Alan, I know. We'll get through this I promise."

Alan kissed her on the cheek and left. He drove to the nearest Publix, picked up Alison's ice cream, and headed home.

CHAPTER 35

Alison

Over the next months, Alison noticed how happy Alan was. She watched him begin to transform a baby's room. With gender neutral colors, Alan, plastered giraffes, trees, birds over yellow hues. She sat next to her husband whom had fallen asleep watching a mystery movie. Gazing at him, Alison, smiled. She was happy too. Their lives seemed to be going well. She continued her therapy and meditated.

"Alan." She nudged him. "Wake up baby."

He wiped his eyes and squinted. "Yeah." He yawned.

"Place your hand here." She guided his hand to her stomach.

Alan sat up. "Is that the baby?"

"It is."

"Alison, I'm so happy. Thank you, baby."

"Thank me, for what?"

He pointed to her stomach. "For this. Our baby. Our legacy."

She kissed him. "Our legacy." She smiled.

Alison led him up the staircase, pointing out areas for portraits of their pending arrival. They giggled and hugged one another.

"Alan." She snuggled up to him. "I would very much like a foot rub and maybe, just maybe if you do it right, I'll let you play around." She winked.

With a wide grin Alan spoke. "Oh, I definitely, believe I can do it right."

***

The Spring daylight creeped between the half open drapes. Alison toward a sleeping Alan. She moved her naked body, stretching a leg over Alan's. Her arm fell around his waist. She sniffed his back. The sport body wash still fresh and intoxicating to her nostrils. Her full breast and erect nipples squeezed between her and him. Her lean finger traced his arm lightly up to his ear. She tightened her leg around his. Alan shifted. Alison was searching for something. Now, on his back, Alison saw exactly what she searched for. Attention it was. Her body hungered for the soldier that stood erect.

"Alison, what are you doing?"

She knew he wasn't asleep for a while. Just playing the role. "I'm doing you?" She straddled him.

"Wow, you didn't get enough last night?" He bucked her.

As long as I can get it, I'm getting it. "She held on."

"I love you baby."

"I love you too."

Around a protruding belly, Alison wrapped her silk robe. She opened the drapes. Beautiful greenery met her. Some red, pink, blue, and yellow flowers were escaping from the buds that held them in all winter. She opened the bedroom double doors to a small balcony and stepped out. Inhaling the morning's brisk air, she smiled.

"I'm going to make us breakfast baby, why don't you have a seat out here and I'll bring it up." Alan swirled her toward him.

"That sounds good. I'll shower then make myself comfortable."

As she sat, rubbing a coconut lotion over her legs, she heard a light ring.

"Hello."

"Alison?"

"Tonya?" Alison wondered why her husband, had Tonya listed as *Drama* for a name.

"Did I call your phone or Alan's?"

"His. Haven't heard from you in a while. You haven't returned my calls and those one-line texts. What's going on?" Alison tapped her fingers against the bamboo chair.

"Girl, too much. Remember I told you Eric wants custody of Asia. After all that none sense he put me through, I need to make some life changes."

"Need to make…what are you doing?"

With a long drawn out breath, "I moved to Chicago."

Alison stood. Moved the phone to her other ear. "What? You moved…already? To Chicago?"

Just as Alison turned, Alan was standing behind her. She pointed to the bamboo chair for him to sit.

She covered the phone. "This is Tonya. She moved to Chicago. Did you know?"

Alan shifted in his seat. Before he could speak, Alison had returned to the conversation.

"Tonya, Alan is here now. Did you tell him you were moving?"

"Well…I did, but it just slipped out. I wasn't going to tell anyone really. That's why I was calling, to let him know I'm all moved in and things are great."

Alison eyes narrowed at Alan. She hmm'd and oh's. "So, Alan was more important for you to tell. You could've text me in one of your one liners."

"You are right Alison. I should've handled things differently. I felt the time was right for me to go. I had a job offer as well; I couldn't pass up the opportunity. May I speak to Alan?"

"You want to speak with Alan?" She looked at Alan. "No, Tonya, I'll give him the message that you're okay."

CHAPTER 36

Alan

The summer was winding down. Football was back. Alan had been in practice for weeks. Being suspended at the end of last season really taught him a lesson. Only, he now has another situation. The next game would be against the Chicago Bears. On their turf. This would be a bitter sweet visit to the Windy City. He missed the birth of his son, but he will have the chance to see him.

Since Tonya last called, he made one final call to her, asking that she text him at a certain time and if…only if he could, he would call. He wasn't trying to disappear from her and his son's life, but biding some time until he could face his wife.

Alan stood in the work out room watching the swirling gray clouds. The winds were beating against the glass door. He watched leaves dance. The tree branches swayed to the wind howling.

"Alan."

With his hands rested on hips, Alan turned. "Yes, baby."

"I don't think she's going to wait another two months."

Alan rushed to Alison. "Are you okay?" He looked her over.

"I'm fine. This baby is anxious. She does a lot of moving and kicking."

"Kicking. Hmm." In a circular motion he rubbed Alison's stomach. "Maybe she'll be football player."

"Um, no she won't."

"Come on Alison. Women play football."

"Don't care. She will not be one of them."

They laughed.

Slowly, he embraced Alison. "I love you baby. I hate to leave you next week."

"I'll be fine. My mom will be here."

"I know you will, but I don't want to leave you ever."

"Are you going to see Tonya when you're in Chicago?"

That was unexpected or was it. Alan knew Alison had to wonder. He avoided any conversation that Tonya may have come up.

He laughed. "Should I see her?"

"I was asking. And no, you shouldn't. I think people come into our lives for a reason and leave for the same."

"I guess you're right." Alan attention went back to the dancing leaves.

"Go ahead and get your work out on. I'm going to lay down for a moment." She kissed his soft lips.

Alan smacked her behind and winked. "I love you Mrs. Perry."

***

"I'm in town. Guess you know that."

"Will you be able to come by? I want you to meet your son."

"Only for a quick second. You know our time is very tight."

"I know it is. This is really awkward."

"What is?" Alan placed his luggage on the bed.

"All this sneaking around and quick phone calls. Not the same before the baby."

"You know this wasn't going to be easy. And I definitely don't need any more news coverage on the negative side. I have to talk to Alison."

"When. When will you do that?"

That was the question he kept asking himself. He didn't know when exactly, but he knew it would happen and soon. The more he dug deeper into this secret the more he felt low down and dirty. Alison didn't deserve what he was going to put her through. He wasn't leaving Alison.

"You seem like it's a bother to you Tonya?"

"No. I think you should tell her because it may ease some of the tension you have."

"Tension? I don't have any tension."

"Okay, you keep believing that."

"I'll try to work on seeing you before I leave."

CHAPTER 37

Alison

"I—I can't do it. I'm tired."

"Mrs. Perry, you're almost there, you can do it. I need one good push from you. The baby's head is here, give us a push and your bundle of joy will make a debut. Mr. Perry, I need you to push her left leg back more."

"Doctor, isn't this enough? She might be hurting."

The doctor winked. "Trust me, Mr. Perry, her leg isn't a concern right now to her. Come on, Mrs. Perry, where's that push…"

Alison took a deep breath, grunted, and pushed. "I'm tired I can't." She inhaled. Do…this." And she exhaled.

"Mrs. Perry, that was good. The baby's shoulders are out and guess what—"

Alan said, "It's our baby girl. Our beautiful baby girl."

"I want to see her." Alison filled with exhaustion, lay back.

Dr. Gibson held the baby while Alan cut the umbilical cord. After Dr. Gibson wiped the baby, he wrapped her in a white blanket and lay her on Alison's chest. For the first time, mom and baby looked at each other.

The nurse removed the baby and did all the preliminary checks. "Your beautiful little girl weighed in at eight pounds and three ounces. I guess she's going to be a tall one...she's twenty-two inches. Well, everything is fine. Her color is good, great oxygen. Here you are, Mom, your bundle of joy."

Alison cuddled their baby girl close to her with Alan close by. A couple of hours passed with nurses in and out checking on Alison.

With blue scrubs and stethoscope peeking from her pocket the nurse said. "Mrs. Perry, I understand you're going to breast feed, correct."

"Yes, that's correct."

"Let's go over the technique. Sometime babies don't latch on properly and it can be very annoying to the mom. Oh my, she's so beautiful. Look at this head full of black curly hair. Now, Mr. Perry, you can watch because it's good to help your wife...a bonding technique for you as well."

Alan nodded.

The nurse assisted with placing the baby in a tucked positioned with the head supported by Alison's hand, the body elongated on her forearm.

"This is easy, Alison, just like holding a football." Alan said.

"Well, she's not a football."

The nurse laughed. "Your husband is right—we do call this position a football hold, but because it feels like you're holding the baby backwards most women prefer to cuddle them in their arms as you're doing."

Alison and Alan marveled over their first born. They vowed to give their baby everything she needed and more. They, however, were very conscious not to spoil the baby, but teach her values and responsibility.

"Do you have a name for your little girl?"

Alison answered, her first name is Adanna, which means father's loving daughter, it's African-Ghana. Her middle name will be Adsila, that's blossom in Cherokee."

"My, you all are quite the family. So much love." The nurse gathered Alison's and the baby's chart. "I'll give you all some time alone."

Alan took a seat and gazed out the enormous window watching the clouds move in a steady direction, while Alison fed their baby. She sang a beautiful lullaby and gently rubbed the baby's face while she continued to feed. Soon she heard light snoring, Alan had fallen asleep.

***

"Mom, how are you?" Alison cradled the phone between her neck and shoulder.

"The question is, how are you? My little baby had a baby of her own." Alison's mom sniffed.

"We're doing fine, Mom. I know you wanted to be here, but she wouldn't wait. You left too soon."

"I'll be back dear. You're not going to go through your first months alone with a newborn. Besides, I want to start spoiling my first grandchild."

Quietness fell over the call. Only Alan's light snoring Alison heard. She looked over to a sleeping Adanna. Alison's eyes scrunched up and she adjusted.

"Mom, are you there?"

"I am. Alison." There was a pause. "What's going on with that girl?"

Alison annoyed. "What girl?"

"Young lady, don't play games with me…the one that wants your husband."

Alison didn't want to go there with her mother. Not on this special occasion. "Tonya moved to Chicago."

"Really?"

"Yes, really. Mom, she doesn't want Alan—"

"Are you comfortable with that girl calling him, popping up at *your* house, he taking her side—"

"Okay, Mom, okay." Alison whispered. "I'm not totally okay with all of that, but I trust my husband. If anything, I would've kept my eyes on her, but no need she's gone."

"Why did she move?"

"She had a job opportunity there and she wanted a change of scenery."

"Well, good for her. Maybe she can find somebody else husband to flirt with. Not that, that's right either."

"No, it isn't right. Mom, I'm trying really hard to keep unnecessary stress out my life. I will not worry about what someone else is or isn't doing as long as it doesn't affect me and mine. I need a peace of mind, especially now for Adanna."

"I hear you baby. Look, one more thing. Your cousin Craig lives in Chicago." Her mother sang out.

"And?"

"If you talk to that girl again, maybe you could steer her his way. He's divorced now."

"Nope. I'm not getting involved. I hadn't heard from Craig in ages. Why didn't we spend time with them, Mom? I would've love to seen uncle and auntie before they passed on."

"Alison, your daddy's brother, Uncle Benny, was something else. He drank and treated your Aunt Geraldine and other women like a dog. That man was awful. He wasn't allowed at my house and I wasn't taking you there."

The gurgle from Adanna caused Alison to raise up and look over in the clear temporary hospital issued bassinet. She reached in and patted the sleeping infant. Oh, joys, a magnificent wonder she and Alan created. How could she have been selfish for so long?

"Alison. What are you doing?"

"Sorry, Mom. Adanna was making noises."

"As I was saying. Craig lives there and it might be good for him to meet a southern girl."

Alison's eye rolled upward. "I have to go. Love you Mom."

CHAPTER 38

Alan

"Great game guys. This was a good one. Winning on home turf. Yeah." The coach pulled his fist in with a high knee. "Bring it in."

The guys huddled in a circle, arms extended, fist closed and on one, two, and three they yelled, "Win, win, yeah, baby." This became a catch on phrase when Alan and Daryl danced and chanted, their way to the locker room during their win over the Chicago Bears.

"Daryl, I need to talk to you." Alan palmed his head.

"What's going on man. You look like someone coming after you?"

Alan whispered. "I fucked up man." Shaking his head, "I'm screwed."

"What?" Daryl looked around the almost empty locker room. "Is it those pictures again?"

"No, none of that. That's nothing compared to what I've done." Still holding his helmet, "Let's talk when we leave."

They walked slowly to the private parking lot of the Mercedes-Benz Stadium, still hearing distant roaring of fans, chant and praise the team on a job well done. Alan stopped short of his vehicle, scanned the parking lot, looking over his shoulder, and faced Daryl.

"Tonya is pregnant. Well, I mean she had the baby...a boy."

"Come again." Daryl placed his hands-on Alan's shoulders. "What did you say?"

"Tonya had my son...a few months ago."

Daryl placed both hands on top of his head. "Good grief, Alan, how did this happen? Does Alison know?"

"No. Not yet. It happened, and I need to come clean with Alison."

"Didn't you use protection?"

"At first, but...anyway, you're the one who told me to hit that."

"Oh, no, don't you blame that on me. I gave you a condom to use. Yes, I said hit that, but not make it a fucking habit. What the hell is wrong with you. If anyone know, you should've kept that wrapped up dog, you're a married man. Geez, fuck."

Alan exhaled. "I know. And I'm sorry for blaming you. I laid in my bed now I have to make it."

"As a matter of fact, I haven't heard you talk about Tonya for a while. Has she been around?"

"She moved to Chicago. I seen my son once. He's beautiful." He smiled.

"Hmm, that's when we had a game against the Bears. You disappeared."

"Yes." Alan picked up his bag, tossed it on the passenger seat. "I have to do, what I have to do. Tell Alison. This isn't going to be easy; I'm scared as hell."

"Sorry about this Alan. In all honesty, you are good guy and I know you love Alison. I shouldn't have opened my big mouth, being that little devil on your shoulder."

Alan stood tall. "See you later Daryl. I have to be a man and go talk to my wife."

Alan snuggly pulled his Nike cap down. Staring at the car display unit, he slowly drove away.

***

The house was quiet. Alan peeked into the dark family room. Dropped his bag. Adjusted the dimmer and sat on the sofa. Arms rested on knees; his head cupped in his hands. He sniffled. Then cried out, "Oh, God. I am so sorry." He glanced around the dim room. Stood with courage. With the back of his strong hands, he wiped his eyes.

Up the staircase he went. Taking two steps at a time. He stopped at the landing. The portraits that appeared to be happy now looked sad. He saw the smiles turned upside down. Adanna, their baby girl, now had her wall space. Beautiful, just like her mother. Wide round brown eyes. A small diamond barrette adorned her big curls. She was Angelic.

He first looked on the sleeping baby. Swaddled in a pink and blue blanket she slept peacefully. Alan finger trailed her temple to cheeks. He kissed her lightly on the forehead. Adanna, gurgled, but kept sleeping.

"Hi Alan."

He turned quickly. "Baby, you scared me." His voice low.

"I've been awake. Heard you on the baby monitor." She gave him a kiss.

Alan looked at Alison. He held her arms and fanned them out. "I love you."

"I love you too."

"I love you so much." He pulled her close. "Alison, I'm sorry."

Alison stepped back. "What's going on Alan?"

He led her to their bedroom. "Sit down." He sat next to her.

"Alan, you're scaring me. What is it?"

"I slept with Tonya and we have a son?" He said it. Just like that.

He held to the area that throbbed. Yes, that was a slap. Alison slapped him. He deserved it.

CHAPTER 39

Alison

Here, they were, in the midnight hour raised voices. Alison paced the room. Tears flowing. She darted toward Alan for another jab in his face only to be stopped by his stance.

"How could you do this to me? To us? She drew an imaginary circle around them. "Alan, I can't believe this. My mother was right—"

He reached for. "Baby, please understand I didn't mean it. I didn't."

Her eyes seem to move one at time, while looking him over. "You didn't mean it. How long has this been going on?"

Alan lowered his head. "Months."

With an upper-cut, she punched him in the mouth. Alan stumbled.

"Months." She shook her hand. "You have a son?" The quiver in her voice concluded another round of tears were coming.

"Alison. Please—"

"How old is he!"

"Two months. Almost three."

"Adanna is one month. Oh, my God, Alan. You were sleeping with both us at the same time." Her head dropped. "And didn't use any protection?"

"—I'm sorry. I'm sorry baby. I didn't mean it. I love you and I am here."

"So, is this why she moved to Chicago? If my math is correct, she was early in her pregnancy. Before the New Year? You two were trying to hide it."

Alan stepped toward her. She stepped back. "Get the hell out. Get out. Get out."

"I-I don't know what you want me to do? What do you mean get out?"

"Alan, I don't want to look at you. I don't want to talk to you. I don't even want to smell your dirty, lying, cheating ass. Get out of this house."

"Alison please, I'll go sleep in another room. I'll stay out of your way. Baby, we don't need speculations and gossip. Please, I'm sorry. Can I stay?"

He looked so pitiful. On his knees, tugging at her robe. How pathetic she thought. Now, he's not so big. She had to admit though, she truly didn't want him to leave, but she didn't want him near her or Adanna.

"Get up. You take your things and go the family room—"

"Family room? I can go in the guest room."

"No. You will stay in the family room. You don't need comfort. That sofa will be just fine for you. If you don't like that option, then get a hotel room?" She smoothed out her robe.

***

"I knew it. I told you to watch that girl—"

The early morning hours crept up on Alison. She knew her mom was an early riser and she did need to hear her voice, if was going to be *I told you so's.* Alison sat quietly. Gliding in the rocker, she breast-fed Adanna, while her mother's voice echoed through the speaker phone. She held her baby close. She inhaled the relaxing lavender scent, that lotioned Adanna. She tucked her finger under Adanna's small hand and let her grip it tightly. She watched her nursing.

"Alison, did you hear what I said."

"Yes, Mother, I did. You were correct." She patted the baby's back.

"What are you going to do about it? If I were you Alan would be out of the house. He doesn't deserve to be there and what—"

Alison gently removed her breast from Adanna's still puckered lips. "Mom, stop it. Please. I will take care of this. As for Alan, I love him. I'm not going to throw my marriage away. Alan is a good man."

"So, you're just going to let that little wrench get away with what she did and him?"

"Shh." She whispered in Adanna's ear. "She's not going to get away with anything. Alan will get his karma. I'm not going to be revengeful and stark crazy. I don't need the stress. My sanity and baby are important to me."

"Alison, I hear you and I love you. I'll be there next week to help you with the baby. Don't expect me to be nice to Alan."

"I love you too Mom. Talk to you later."

She knew her mom was stubborn, but she would get over it. Alison stood. She looked out to the Koi pond and beautiful landscaping surrounding it. She loved the facets of colors. The sun, at full glow, was emitting warm rays she could feel on the window. She lay the cooing infant on her shoulder and patted Adanna's back. Slowly, she circled the room, continuing to pat until she heard a belching sound. Alison, looked at Adanna, making sure there were no puke. Then she heard a light burp from the baby's pamper. Alison laughed. Kissed her baby and returned to the glide rocker.

Did her mother really think she would let Tonya get away with it? Alison, wasn't going to let her therapy sessions of improving herself and quality of life go out the window. Her and Alan first have to recover. Only, until then, can she and him together decide how to deal with Tonya and her son.

CHAPTER 40

Alan

Alan stood at the staircase and looked up. He was happy that he still saw Adanna every day he was home. She was accessible as long as Alison wasn't feeding, bathing, or bonding with her. Which seem to be all the time. However, he hadn't shared a bed with his wife in a month. With his away games and banishment to the family room he felt lonely. Being in the same home was taking a toll on him. He only saw Alison a few times, when he made excuses to get personal items from their bedroom. She had made it clear to him to give her space.

When her mother came to visit. Alan, was thrilled he would be there for one day and that was enough. His mother-in-law, made it a point to visit the family room and chat.

He recalled that moment. "Look, Ma—" He stood to greet her.

"I'm going to be nice for my daughter."

"I apologized to Alison. I sincerely am sorry. I apologize to you as well. I was disrespectful when you were here last year. I am sorry."

"How long have I known you Alan? A long, long time."

"Yes, you have."

"I'm disappointed in you. I have always loved you. My daughter loves you dearly. She always has. I remember she worked at that diner.

That was all to impress you and help pay her way to college. She wanted to be with you."

A smile eased on Alan's face. "I know she did. I'm going to make this right."

"How, Alan, how?"

"Whatever my wife wants me to do."

"Alan." His mother-in-law approached. "Make it right, son. I know you're a great husband, despite what has happened and you're a great father. You two are young. You can get over this." She hugged him.

His eyes wide. He didn't know how to respond. Although, she was never nasty to him, until Tonya came into the picture. He does blame himself for everything. It was all him. He should have said no, the first time and got his ass out of Tonya's house.

***

Pastor Beauridge, understood the football player's hectic schedule and worked with Alan on Pastoral counseling when possible. He took Alison's suggestion to have the counseling. If he was home for a week, he went at least two times. The pastor, dedicated, to Alan's absolution offered phone check-ins and daily scriptures emailed.

"You want me to journal?" Alan flinched. "That's girlish."

"Alan." The pastor words were slow. "You would enjoy it. Nothing girlish about journaling. Jot down what has happened. Then look back on what you wrote?"

"Pastor, sound girlish to me."

The Pastor laughed. "Indeed. Take time to meditate on what you wrote. Note how you feel."

"Journaling can't hurt. If I have to include this in my redemption, then so be it. I have been here for weeks now and I realize, Pastor, my actions were based on hurt. When Alison told me, she didn't want a baby and then I caught her taking her birth control pills, I was upset."

"And you felt going outside your marriage was the way to handle your anger?"

"Well." He glanced at the floor. "At the time being angry, it was. Yes, I was attracted to the other woman." He kept Tonya anonymity.

"How do you feel about it now."

He shook his head. "Oh, I feel terrible. I could have given Alison a disease. She may have left me. Not fair to her. None of this was fair to her."

"Alan, you have to apologize to the other woman and find a way to be a part of the baby's life, with Alison. She must be included."

"I will Pastor."

Alan stood, extending his hand. "Pastor, I will be in church as soon as my schedule allows, with my family."

CHAPTER 41

Alison

"Alan come here please." She yelled into the family room.

Alison busied herself about the kitchen. A skillet on the stove held an inch of water with sliced baby carrots. She measured out a cup of brown sugar, two tablespoons of salted butter, and half cup of orange zest.

"Hey, baby, what's up?" Alan held a black notebook.

Wiping her hands on the white apron, trimmed in red, with her initials in gold letters centered in the middle, she smiled. "How are you doing? How have your counseling been going?"

"I love it. Pastor is great. A few more sessions and—"

"I want you to move back in the room with me. I believe it's time to be a family. A real family."

Alan hugged her. "Thank you, baby."

"But first, we need to discuss Tonya." She turned to the boiling carrots. "We have to be adults and accept what has happened and move on." She sighed heavily.

"I know baby, I know. This won't be easy for you. I truly am sorry for what I did. I am thankful that you didn't leave me." His hands slipped around her waist.

"No, this won't be easy, but we will get through it. She put a colander in the sink and drained the carrots. "Alan." She dumped the sugar and rest of the ingredients into the skillet and stirred. "After dinner we will call Tonya and talk about this."

"Of course, baby. Whatever you need me to do, I will."

She continued to stir the mixture and gave Alan a sideways look. "Thank you, baby."

Alison dropped the carrots into the hot bubbly mixture and coating them well. She sat the steamed broccoli, and baked fish on the table. Once the carrots were done, she put them in a serving bowl and drizzled the remaining sauce on top.

After looking in on a sleeping Adanna, Alison returned to the kitchen. Alan stood behind her chair.

"After you, he pulled the chair out."

Alison took the apron off, tossed it on the counter and took her awaiting seat. "Thank you, sir."

They smiled. Alison was quiet. She gave Alan her undivided attention as he rambled on about his discoveries in journaling. She took hold of his hand.

"I love you Alan. I'm sorry as well.

"Why are you sorry?"

"I know I may have been a little unpredictable with my attitude, mood swings, or selfishness. I should have been more open with you about having a baby. I left it open ended, so naturally, one would assume that their desire would be met. Sorry."

"It's okay. Let's enjoy dinner. Thank you for this."

***

"Hello, Tonya, how are you?" Alison dryly said.

"Alison? Oh, I'm well."

"Tonya, you are on speaker. Alan is here too."

"Hey, Tonya."

"Alan."

Alison took lead. "We are calling to discuss what we can do with Alan and I participating in the baby's…his son's life."

"I…I never thought that you would want to be a part of this."

"Really, Tonya. Alan is *my* husband and we are doing this together. He's not leaving me and his daughter. I'm trying to be an adult about this. You are a single mother raising two children now. I know it's hard. Even though, what you two did was wrong, the baby shouldn't have to suffer. Alan, will take care of his financial responsibility."

"I've told Alan, he doesn't have to be a part of this baby's life. You know, if he could from time to time help out. I don't want to cause any more problems."

"Too late for that." Alison looked at Alan. "Adanna has a big brother…by a few months." She gasped. "They need to know each other."

Alan chimed in. "Yes, Tonya, Bradley need to know his sister."

Tonya's sniffles echoed. "Thank you, Alison…Alan." A baby's cry, softly, crept in.

"This will be work for all of us. And Tonya." Alison then looked at Alan. "We will work this out for visitation as well. Us visiting you, you visiting us. I'm definitely not saying this will happen overnight."

Now, the distance cry was louder. "Thank you, both of you. I have to feed Bradley. Thank you."

"We will talk later. Take care of the baby." Alison said.

"Kiss my son for me." Alan looked at Alison. She looked away.

She grabbed the baby monitor. She took Alan's hand. They sat at the lighted Koi pond. The night air was cool. Quietness swept through the misty grass. Leaves fading colors, rustled on the trees.

"I love you Alison."

"I love you too, Mr. Perry. I love you too." Alison leaned toward him.

Their eyes searched back and forth. Alison kissed her husband. She listened to Adanna's intermittent sounds through the monitor. She was happy. You only live once and you have to make the best of it.

The End